I0591879

Money Matters

Michael Parker
and Susan Parker

A Samuel French Acting Edition

SAMUEL
FRENCH
FOUNDED 1830

SAMUELFRENCH.COM
SAMUELFRENCH-LONDON.CO.UK

FOR PRODUCTION ENQUIRIES

UNITED STATES AND CANADA
Info@SamuelFrench.com
1-866-598-8449

UNITED KINGDOM AND EUROPE
Plays@SamuelFrench-London.co.uk
020-7255-4302

Each title is subject to availability from Samuel French, depending upon country of performance. Please be aware that MONEY MATTERS may not be licensed by Samuel French in your territory. Professional and amateur producers should contact the nearest Samuel French office or licensing partner to verify availability.

MUSIC USE NOTE

Licensees are solely responsible for obtaining formal written permission from copyright owners to use copyrighted music in the performance of this play and are strongly cautioned to do so. If no such permission is obtained by the licensee, then the licensee must use only original music that the licensee owns and controls. Licensees are solely responsible and liable for all music clearances and shall indemnify the copyright owners of the play(s) and their licensing agent, Samuel French, against any costs, expenses, losses and liabilities arising from the use of music by licensees. Please contact the appropriate music licensing authority in your territory for the rights to any incidental music.

IMPORTANT BILLING AND CREDIT REQUIREMENTS

If you have obtained performance rights to this title, please refer to your licensing agreement for important billing and credit requirements.

MONEY MATTERS was first produced by the Main Street Players of Boone County, Community Building Complex of Boone County, Belvedere, Illinois on February 13, 2015. The Designer was Lon Hoegberg and the Director was John B. Van Nest. The cast was as follows:

GEORGE	Pete Gulatto
ANNIE	Dawn Stroup
MARILENA	Jenni Minarik
CHARMAINE	Denise Gorski
BUD	Ronn Gordon
BERNARD	Keith Burritt
SECOND GHOST	Skyler Melillo

TIME

The Present

PLACE

Monet Manor. A Country Mansion… Somewhere USA.

ACT I: A late summer afternoon.
ACT II: The action is continuous.

CHARACTERS

GEORGE – (Age 50+) A kind, good natured soul who has worked almost twenty years for the owners of Monet Manor, Mr. Hammond, who passed away ten years ago and his widow who passed away two weeks ago. He works in the basement printing twenty dollar bills on an old press built many years ago by Mr. Hammond. He is a gentle person, who is, perhaps, influenced too much by his daughter Annie. He has given little thought to the fact that what he is doing is wrong, probably because he feels he is not harming anyone. He is a total hypochondriac, with every ailment imaginable, *(and some unimaginable).* At first, flattered by Charmaine's attentions *(His daughter's friend),* he begins to realize that he is attracted to their neighbor Marilena, which eventually evolves into a tender love story. *(Caring, thoughtful,* always *the gentleman)*

ANNIE – (Age 30+) George's daughter. A take charge type, who is probably responsible for the fact that they have gotten away with their counterfeiting year after year, by rigidly following the credo of Mr. Hammond. She is totally lacking in any sense of humor, but continues to listen patiently to George's jokes, which she never understands. When the manor is unexpectedly bequeathed to a stranger, Bud Davis, she cooks up a plot to persuade him to sell the manor to her and George. When things begin to fall apart, it is Annie who keeps her cool and finds a way out of their predicament. *(Competent, resourceful, quick thinking)*

MARILENA – (Age 50+) The neighbor of George and Annie, Marilena is a self-professed psychic. She is The Contesa de Buzau Si Severin from Transylvania, but George refers to her as "The Romanian Fruitcake". She speaks with an accent and occasionally uses Romanian phrases. Her flamboyant personality shines through in manner, dress and movement. She speaks to spirits, and feels the presence of "money" when visiting George and Annie. She is overwhelmed by the attention given to her by "Bud the Stud" Davis, but can she deny her feelings for George? *(Flamboyant, mysterious, eccentric)*

CHARMAINE – (Age 30+) An old college friend and sorority sister of Annie's, she is the quintessential Southern Belle. She is beautiful and voluptuous, with an over active libido. On principle she puts a move on all men. As an actress, she has been invited to Monet Manor by Annie to play the role of a ghost, in order to convince Mr. Davis the house is haunted. She quickly realizes that she knows who Davis is, and admits that she had an affair with him years before, and dumped him because he was two-timing her. She embraces her role, eager to help her friend and to thwart the plans of Davis. *(Out going, gushing, demonstrative)*

BUD DAVIS – (Age 60+) The current owner of Monet Manor, which was bequeathed to him by Mrs. Hammond, a former paramour. He has little interest in Annie and George's proposal to purchase the manor from him, and never really believes that it is "haunted." Bud's intention for the Manor is to convert it into a retirement home for women, which will only further his hobby, sex. Bud sees himself as a geriatric sex machine, who is more interested in his next conquest then the cash Annie and George are prepared to offer him. *(Slight and frail, charismatic, brazen but likeable)*

BERNARD – (Age 30+) A freelance property appraiser and design consultant hired by Bud to do a cost analysis on the feasibility of turning the Manor into a retirement home for women. He appears to be very motivated by money and making deals. He is never far from his cell phone and becomes very secretive at times. When he discovers the printing press, he forces George and Annie into a deal. At first there appears little they can do to protect themselves from his evil intentions, but in the end, with Charmaine's help, the tables are turned on him. *(Mercenary, self-involved, unscrupulous)*

ACT I

(It is a late summer afternoon in the main reception room of Monet Manor, Somewhere U.S.A. Monet Manor was owned by the recently deceased widow, Hilda Hammond. Downstage left is an open archway leading to the front entrance. Above it is a table with two chairs, and above that, on the left wall, is a pair of French doors leading to the garden, and **MARILENA**'s house. *Downstage right is a small bedroom, converted from an office. In the bedroom is a double bed with side tables. Above the bed is a door to a bathroom. Upstage of the bedroom door is a double hinged door to the kitchen and basement. The entire upstage area is a platform, with a railing, raised perhaps two steps in the center, with an exit left leading to other parts of the manor. Left will be* **ANNIE**'s, **GEORGE**'s, *and* **BERNARD**'s *rooms. Center is a bookcase at least six feet tall and five feet wide. It swivels on a hidden central post. On it are books and a personal computer. On each side of the bookcase is a bedroom door. The right is guest room one, and will be* **CHARMAINE**'s. *The left is guest room two and will be* **BUD**'s. *Center right in the living room is a couch and chair, with a small end table between them.)*

(As the curtain rises, **ANNIE** *is sitting at the table.* **ANNIE** *is age 30+ and a take-charge type who tends to boss her father around. She does not have a great sense of humor, as we shall see. She is rapidly counting out money and putting it into piles. She is dressed casually in a blouse, and either blue jeans or blue jean skirt. The table is covered with stacks of one, five and ten dollar bills in bundles with rubber bands around them. There should appear to be about eighty thousand dollars on the table.)*

ANNIE. *(Rapidly counting like an experienced bank teller.)* Ten, twenty, thirty, forty, fifty, sixty, seventy, eighty, ninety, one-hundred. *(Places the bills in a stack on the table and grabs another handful out of a bag next to her on the floor. This bag should be quite distinctive in design and color with the Greek letters Delta Mu embroidered on it.)* Ten, twenty, thirty, forty, fifty…

(Enter **GEORGE** *from the kitchen with an oil can in his hand.* **GEORGE** *is 60-ish and is wearing a checkered shirt, overalls, work boots, and a tool belt. He is easy going, with a wry sense of humor. A "gentle" soul, who doesn't see that what he is doing is criminal. He believes it doesn't really hurt anyone.)*

GEORGE. Hi Annie.

ANNIE. *(Doesn't stop counting.)* Hi Dad, eighty, ninety, one-hundred. *(Stops and places the pile on the table.)*

GEORGE. *(Moves left.)* So, how much did we net on your trip to Boston?

ANNIE. I haven't quite finished counting, but it looks to be almost the same as the eighty-five thousand we printed last month.

GEORGE. Way to go.

ANNIE. It was a good trip, but we've still got to make the most of what little time we may have left. We always assumed Mrs. Hammond would leave us the house when she died and we would be able to go on working the printing press forever. What in heaven's name made her change her mind and leave the house to this Bud Davis guy and not us, I will never understand.

GEORGE. I have to admit it was a shocker when we read the will. After all, Mr. Hammond said he'd always take care of us, and Mrs. Hammond said the same after he died. I always assumed it meant leaving us the house.

ANNIE. What could she have been thinking? She knew about the printing press. Do you suppose she told him about it?

GEORGE. Who? That Davis guy? I don't think she was that foolish. Maybe she thought leaving us the rest of her money was better than the house.

ANNIE. Lot of good that does us. If we had the press we wouldn't need the money. Are you absolutely sure we can't move it?

GEORGE. That's impossible, Mr. Hammond built it thirty years ago, it weighs over a thousand pounds, and it's built in behind a fake brick wall in the basement.

ANNIE. Well if this Davis guy finds it we would be in huge trouble. That's why we have to persuade him to sell us the house. We've got enough money saved up, especially after this last trip.

GEORGE. Tell me again exactly what this Bud Davis said to you when you spoke to him on the phone last week.

ANNIE. Not a whole lot, except he wants to turn the manor into a retirement home for ladies. He is not interested in selling at all, he's hired some sort of designer or architect to advise him about the changes he'll have to make, and they're both coming here later today.

GEORGE. OK then let's get all this cleaned up in case he arrives early. *(Sits at the table and grabs a handful of bills and starts to laboriously count.)* Ten, *(Pauses.)*, twenty, *(Pauses.)*…

ANNIE. *(Reaches over and takes the money from him.)* Dad please, you do the printing I'll do the passing…and the counting. *(She continues to count.)* Thirty, forty, fifty… *(Quietly finishes and rubber bands the stack.)*

GEORGE. Sure, sure…you get to have all the fun. You traipse all over the country visiting exciting, major cities, while I'm stuck in a dirty, stinky basement working that old printing press getting ink all over my hands. Do you have any idea of how long it takes to get the watermarks on the paper just right? It's terribly hard on my hands. You know I have rheumatoid arthritis, and a constant back ache from working that old press, then there's my bunions…have I told you lately about my bunions?

ANNIE. Not since yesterday Dad, and it's not as glamorous as you think. It's hard work spending eighty-five thousand dollars. It took me three weeks to get rid of all those fake twenties. It's not like I can go and buy a thousand dollar painting and pay for it with twenties and then return it the next day. Stores that give cash refunds are getting harder and harder to find. I sometimes wish we could print fifties and hundreds.

GEORGE. Ah, just remember Mr. Hammond's credo: First, never print more than a twenty, because no one ever checks twenties, and second, never use one of them in your own home town. That's why we've been able to get away with it for ten years, and Mr. Hammond was able to do it for twenty years prior to that.

ANNIE. I know, I know…it's the credo we live by and if we're going to continue to live this lifestyle then Mr. Davis has to be persuaded to sell us the manor.

GEORGE. Annie, indulge me, explain again how this weekend is going to work.

ANNIE. Sure Dad. When we got the phone call from Mr. Davis saying he intends to turn this manor into a retirement home for women, I knew that our first option was to make him a huge offer to buy the house, but he wouldn't even listen. So, I figured that if we could convince him it was haunted, he'd give up his idea of turning it into a retirement home, and then we could buy it. That's why I've invited my old friend, and sorority sister, Charmaine Beauregard, to come here and play the role of a ghost. She's a retired actress and says she is more than happy to help me out.

GEORGE. Where did you ever get the idea of a ghost?

ANNIE. From our neighbor, Marilena. She claims to have psychic powers and she's always going on about how she feels presences in the manor.

GEORGE. Oh you mean the Romanian Fruitcake.

ANNIE. Dad! I know you really like her a lot and she really is The Contesa Marilena de Buzau Si Severin. *[See Authors' Notes.]*

GEORGE. That's what I said, The Romanian Fruitcake. Seriously, you don't believe in any of that spirit stuff do you?

ANNIE. No Dad, I don't, but some people do.

GEORGE. But a ghost? Are you sure this is going to work?

ANNIE. It will when Charmaine looks like one and disappears into the wall. Now, have you wired up the dimmer switches?

GEORGE. Yep.

ANNIE. Is the bookcase working properly? *(Starts to silently count out another pile and rubber band it.)*

GEORGE. *(Moves upstage to the bookcase with the oil can.)* Let me just check it out. It has to be smooth and silent. *(Turns it.)* Maybe just a drop of oil on the pivot. *(He then tests the turn-table.)* It's pretty smooth. *(He closes the bookcase and turns down stage, clutches his tummy and moans and groans, then doubles over on the rail.)*

ANNIE. *(Looks up.)* Dad, whatever are you doing?

GEORGE. Resting.

ANNIE. Resting?

GEORGE. Resting. You know I almost have a ruptured spleen.

ANNIE. Dad, there's nothing wrong with your spleen.

GEORGE. I know, that's why I said almost.

ANNIE. *(Grabs another handful of bills from the bag.)* Come on Dad, we've got Charmaine, the designer fellow and Mr. Davis all coming later today, we have to make sure everything is ready. We don't have time for your shenanigans. *(Starts to count.)* Ten, twenty, thirty, forty…

GEORGE. Annie, *(Comes down left to the table.)* Did I ever tell you the story of the boy ghost and the girl ghost?

ANNIE. No Dad, but I know you're going to. *(Places the last pile in a stack and starts to gather them up and rubber bands them together.)*

GEORGE. *(Now behind the table.)* OK. The boy ghost says to the girl ghost, "What are you doing tonight?" She says, "Are you trying to pick me up?" He says, "Yes, but you always seem to slip through my fingers." Then the girl ghost says, "Oh, you're so transparent, and it's not going to work." And the boy ghost says, "Why not?" She says, "Because I can see right through you."

*(There is a long pause as **ANNIE** looks at him.)*

ANNIE. I don't get it. Of course she can see through him, he's a ghost.

GEORGE. It's not supposed to be…oh never mind.

(The doorbell rings.)

ANNIE. I'll put the money away while you get the door.

*(**GEORGE** crosses left to the entrance, while **ANNIE** pushes the stacks of money into the sorority bag. She places it on the floor behind her chair and moves center stage.)*

*(**CHARMAINE** enters from the down left entrance way, followed by **GEORGE** carrying her suitcase. He stops just inside the entrance way and puts the bag down. **CHARMAINE** age 30+, is a true southern belle, complete with femme fatale southern charm. Her libido is most definitely working and never stops. She is wearing an elegant, low cut summer dress with matching purse, high heel shoes, and is carrying a sorority bag identical to **ANNIE**'s.)*

ANNIE. *(cont.)* *(Steps forward to hug* **CHARMAINE**.*)* Charmaine, it's been far too long. Why you haven't changed one bit, I see you still have your old sorority bag. Me too, I still use mine.

CHARMAINE. Annie, it's great to see you. I agree, it's been far too long.

ANNIE. I'm so glad you're here. Let's sit down. *(Motions for her to sit on the couch.)* I see you met my dad, George.

CHARMAINE. *(Sits on couch left side.)* Annie you never told me you had such a handsome hunk for a father. Why! I think he's just the tomcat's kitten.

GEORGE. *(Visibly flustered, picks up* **CHARMAINE**'s *suitcase.)* Annie, where do you want Charmaine's bag?

ANNIE. In the guestroom. Thanks Dad.

GEORGE. OK, I'll be in the basement if you need me. Nice to meet you Charmaine.

(He crosses left, picks up the bag of money, the oil can and goes upstage and drops the suitcase in bedroom one, then exits to the kitchen.)

CHARMAINE. The pleasure's all mine. Now don't you be gone too long honey lamb.

ANNIE. *(Crosses to the chair.)* Charmaine, you really haven't changed. You wouldn't be putting a move on my dad, would you?

CHARMAINE. Well, older men have more to offer.

ANNIE. Just not as often.

CHARMAINE. Why he's cuter than a sack full of puppies, but don't y'all worry, it's just habit. I just can't help myself.

(Enter **MARILENA** *through the French doors. She is age 50-ish and a Romanian gypsy type. She is wearing a peasant blouse and long skirt, sandals, and has a scarf around her head, tied to the side. Her outfit is flamboyant with bright colors. Despite her somewhat unorthodox manner and dress, she is in fact a very handsome woman, almost beautiful in a mysterious sort of way. Her movements are always flowing and graceful, as if she is floating rather than walking. From the French doors we see her head peak around and into the room. She speaks with a Romanian accent.)*

MARILENA. *(In a sing-song voice.)* Hellooooo.

ANNIE. Hello Marilena.

MARILENA. *(Steps into the room.)* Buna seara, *[See Authors' Notes.]* Annie.

(Takes a few steps towards center stage then suddenly stops and slowly spins around arms outstretched, totally ignoring **ANNIE** *and* **CHARMAINE.***)*

The vibrations, the vibrations... I feel a presence in this room.

CHARMAINE. Why, she must mean me, I often have that affect on people, but it's usually men.

MARILENA. *(Now moving right.)* The vibrations, they're very strong today... I'm sensing something... *(She opens the door of the bedroom and looks in and stays in the doorway.)* Ooh, there is something or someone here. What is this room?

ANNIE. Well, it used to be an office, but a few weeks before Mrs. Hammond passed away, she was having difficulty negotiating steps, and we turned it into a little bedroom for her. We just haven't had time to change it back.

MARILENA. Perhaps it is her presence I feel. No, no, no... *(She pauses, gasps, turns and sweeps into the living room.)* Wait, there is more...money...money, it has to do with money. *(She moves down left and places her hands on the top of the table.)* Much money...

ANNIE. *(Quickly moves towards* **MARILENA** *who appears to be in a momentary trance.)* Marilena please come and sit down and meet my friend.

*(***ANNIE*** is almost pulling* **MARILENA** *towards the couch.)*

Marilena, this is my friend, Charmaine Beauregard.

CHARMAINE. *(Stands and offers to shake* **MARILENA***'s hand.)* Pleasure to meet you.

MARILENA. *(Acknowledges* **CHARMAINE** *with a slight head bow.)* The spirits, they are restless, they call me, I must go now. Please excuse me. *La revedere [See Authors' Notes.]*

(She floats across the room and exits through the French doors.)

CHARMAINE. *(Sits back down on the couch.)* Who or what was that?

ANNIE. *(Closing the French doors left open by* **MARILENA***.)* That was the Contesa Marilena de Buzau Si Severin from Transylvania, our new neighbor.

CHARMAINE. She acts like she fell out of the loony tree and hit every branch on the way down, bless her heart.

ANNIE. *(Stands behind the chair, laughing.)* My Dad calls her the Romanian Fruitcake, she's a bit extreme, but harmless enough. She claims to be a psychic medium. After the new owner arrives, I've asked her to hold a séance later today, and that's where you come in, you're going to play the role of the ghost.

CHARMAINE. Slow down, you'd better explain to me what this is all about.

(Enter **GEORGE** *from the kitchen.)*

ANNIE. *(Stands.)* Hi Dad, good timing. Why don't you explain how the ghost and the bookshelf are going to work, while I go and fix us a snack. I leave you in capable hands Charmaine. *(Exits to the kitchen.)*

CHARMAINE. *(Stands.)* Why Georgie, why don't you come on down here and sit right next to little ol' Charmaine and tell me exactly what it is you want me to do. *(Sits and pats the seat next to her.)*

GEORGE. *(Moves down to the couch and sits about two feet to her left.)* Well there's not much to tell really, you're a ghost.

CHARMAINE. *(Moves left a little closer to* **GEORGE** *and he moves a little further left, keeping the space between them.)* What will I be wearing?

GEORGE. Well, a sheet I guess, don't all ghosts wear sheets?

CHARMAINE. *(Moves a little closer as he moves further away.)* Why I don't know Georgie, I've never been a ghost before, but I sure do like the idea of wearing nothin' but a sheet.

GEORGE. Nothin'?

CHARMAINE. *(Moves a little closer.)* Nothin' at all.

> *(**GEORGE** tries to move away, but has no where to go and eventually is tottering on the arms edge of the couch.)*

Georgie, are you all right?

> *(She tries to grab him to steady him, but ends up falling backwards onto the couch with **GEORGE** on top of her.)*

Oh my!

GEORGE. I'm so sorry. *(Gets up.)* I think perhaps I'd better show you the bookshelf.

CHARMAINE. Now that's a line I haven't heard before. O.K. Georgie, show me the bookshelf.

GEORGE. *(Heads up stage and stops by the bookshelf, followed by **CHARMAINE**.)* This bookshelf is on a swivel in the middle and when you're the ghost, this is where you're going to disappear. Annie says, if the lights are right, it will look like you went straight through the wall. By the way, the other side of the bookshelf is the closet in your room.

CHARMAINE. Well bless my stars and garters, you can come through my wall anytime Georgie Porgie. Why don't you show me how it works. *(**GEORGE** opens the bookcase.)* Where do I go?

GEORGE. Follow me, I'll show you.

> *(He goes in the right side of the bookcase. **CHARMAINE** follows. There is a loud off stage "Who.o.o.o.o" from **GEORGE**, who then appears on the left side of the bookcase with **CHARMAINE**'s hands firmly grabbing his derriere.)*

> *(**ANNIE** Enters from the kitchen with a tray of sandwiches and a pot of coffee and mugs, just in time to see **GEORGE** enter and disappear back into the right side of the bookcase the second time.)*

ANNIE. Oh, good, Dad…

(She watches as they go around with CHARMAINE *still attached to* GEORGE*'s derierre…*GEORGE *continues his "Who.o.o.o" noises.)*

You're showing Charmaine the bookshelf.

(They reappear.)

Dad???…

(She watches as they go around a third time. She quickly puts the tray down on the end table, and runs up the stairs to the bookcase. As they reappear she grabs GEORGE *by the arm and pulls him forward, followed by* CHARMAINE*.)*

ANNIE. *(cont.)* What's going on here?

CHARMAINE. *(Quickly lets go of* GEORGE*'s derriere.)* It was dark in there, I was just feeling my way around.

ANNIE. Feeling your way around? Dad?

GEORGE. Er…er…

CHARMAINE. George was going too fast and I got a little behind. *(Starts to giggle.)*

ANNIE. A little behind? Dad?

GEORGE. Well, it was definitely a hands-on experience.

ANNIE. Dad, for heavens sakes, close the bookshelf and come and sit down, I made some coffee. I need to fill Charmaine in on what's going to happen tonight.

*(*CHARMAINE *comes down and sits on the couch right side.* GEORGE *follows close behind her, intending to sit next to her. He sees* ANNIE *looking at him and quickly sits in the chair while* ANNIE *stands behind the table and pours the coffee. She then hands a mug to* CHARMAINE *and* GEORGE*, then sits on the couch left side.)*

CHARMAINE. Annie, you never did tell me who Mrs. Hammond left the house to.

ANNIE. A Mr. Bud Davis.

CHARMAINE. That name sounds very familiar. Who is he?

GEORGE. We don't know.

CHARMAINE. You mean you've never met him?

ANNIE. He's never been here. I guess she met him on one of her trips. It was really strange though, because in the will she referred to him as her Budly, Studly, Do-right.

CHARMAINE. *(Leaps to her feet and says in a slow, loud deliberate voice.)* Oh, my dear Lord, I think I know him.

ANNIE & GEORGE. WHAT?

CHARMAINE. It's Bud the stud.

ANNIE & GEORGE. Bud the stud?

CHARMAINE. Bud the stud.

ANNIE. How do you know him?

CHARMAINE. It was a few years ago, when I was on vacation.

ANNIE. What happened?

CHARMAINE. Well he's quite a charmer and I succumbed to his charms.

ANNIE. Now Charmaine, be honest, who was chasing who?

CHARMAINE. Well, perhaps it was a little bit of both, but when I found out he was chasing after two other women, at the same time, in the same house, well…

ANNIE. *(Laughing.)* That seems a bit much, even for you.

CHARMAINE. Bud was behaving like a rooster on a hen house roof.

GEORGE. But why would he want to turn this manor into a retirement home for women?

CHARMAINE. Oh my Granny's garters, that's it! *(Pauses.)* Why, that little weasel is trying to create his own personal harem. Give him a chance he'll be busier than a one legged man in a butt kicking contest.

ANNIE. Now I understand why he wouldn't even listen to an offer to buy the place.

CHARMAINE. Well, I can tell you that Mr. Bud Davis is not interested in money, only sex. We call his brain Mr. Zipper.

ANNIE. Oh, dear, so, do you think my idea of holding a séance to convince him it's haunted will work?

CHARMAINE. Knowing him, he'll probably try to seduce the ghost, but we all know that's not going to happen.

GEORGE. *(Looking at* CHARMAINE.*)* Are you sure?

ANNIE. DAD!

CHARMAINE. Georgie, my engine may be running, but I can assure you that my front wheel drive is only aimed at one man at a time.

ANNIE. CHARMAINE!

GEORGE. But how can we be sure it will work?

CHARMAINE. To knock him off his perch, I will give the performance of a lifetime. Why, that little skunk will rue the day he messed with a Beauregard. Believe me, it will work. So, if you'll excuse me, I need to go and prepare for my starring role in tonight's play... Bud the Stud's Last Stand. *(Exits to bedroom one.)*

ANNIE. I forgot what a character she is.

GEORGE. Speaking of characters, did I ever tell you the story of the baby that was born without ears?

ANNIE. No Dad, but I have a feeling you're about to.

GEORGE. OK. There's this couple and the wife is telling the husband that her sister has given birth to a baby without any ears, and they're going 'round there tonight and she doesn't want him to mention that the baby has no ears. The husband says, of course I won't. The wife says, I know you, you'll find a way. Anyway, they get around to her sisters and they're all looking at the baby. The husband says, how's its nose? The mother says, it's perfect, look at that little button of a nose. The husband says, how's its mouth? The mother says, it's perfect, look at that cherub mouth. The husband says, how's its eyes? The mother says, perfect, look at those big, blue eyes. The husband says, well that's good, 'cause it isn't ever going to wear glasses, is it?

ANNIE. *(Long pause.)* I don't get it. Why would it have to wear glasses if its eyes were perfect?

GEORGE. Don't you see... Oh never mind. I'm going to go lie down for awhile. All that work in the closet has worn me out, my sciatica is really starting to flare up again.

ANNIE. You've never had sciatica Dad.

GEORGE. Who are you going to believe, me or those doctors? *(Exits up left.)*

ANNIE. Always you Dad, always you. *(Exits to kitchen.)*

(Enter MARILENA who has been waiting outside the French doors for the room to be empty. She floats around the room, once again "checking for vibrations and spirits", which she felt earlier.)

MARILENA. I must make sure the room is cleansed for tonight. That the spirits will accept our eagerness to communicate with them. Oh my, I am feeling a strong presence.

(BUD knocks on the front door.)

Yes spirits, I hear you, I am here. The presence, it grows stronger.

(BUD knocks louder.)

I hear you oh spirits, what do you need, what do you want?

(BUD knocks again.)

Spirits?...

(One more knock from BUD. She looks around, but sees no one.)

Oh, it's the front door.

(She exits briefly down left to answer the front door returning immediately with BUD.)

(BUD is a slight frail looking man, age perhaps 60+. BUD only ever has one thing on his mind...his next conquest. He is wearing a short sleeve plaid shirt and

*khaki pants, which are pulled up high on his waist, a
sweater vest and a golf cap. He is carrying an overnight
bag which he puts down just to the right of the down left
table.)*

BUD. I have never seen such a vision of loveliness, such
beauty, such charm. I have dreamed of love many
times in my life, but the face in my dreams was never
as beautiful as the one I see before me now.

MARILENA. *(Looks around the room to see who he's talking to,
then realizes it's her.)* Me?

BUD. I see no other vision before me.

MARILENA. You too see visions?

BUD. Only the figure I see before me, the smile, the grace,
the unparalleled beauty of a woman...

MARILENA. O *doamne,* *[See Authors' Notes.]* *(My goodness!)*

BUD. Oh yes, you have the face that launched a thousand
ships, Helen of Troy, you have the body of the Venus
de Milo, and clearly the mind and spirit of Cleopatra.

MARILENA. Cleopatra? Oh, the spirits must be playing
games with me.

BUD. *(To himself.)* I know one spirit who'd like to play with
you.

MARILENA. Sir, I am honored by your words, but I am
merely the Contesa Marilena de Buzau Si Severin,
Annie's neighbor, and you are?

BUD. *(With a slight bow.)* Bud Davis, at your service Madam.

MARILENA. Your words are like magic, you have a gift...

BUD. Gift! I have in my car, French wine and Swiss
chocolates which will be my gift to the beautiful vision
I see before me.

MARILENA. You travel with French wine and Swiss
chocolates?

BUD. Of course, I don't leave home without them. I shall
return. *(Exits the front door.)*

(Left alone on stage, **MARILENA** *takes a few steps towards the front door, as if she is drawn towards* **BUD**. *She stops and blows kisses after him.)*

MARILENA. *Aoleu, ('Oh my'.) [See Authors' Notes.]* who is that enchanting man? *(Twirls and clutches her hands to her heart.)* Be still my beating heart. Spirits, you have brought me a man, no not a man, a God-like creature, whose words are music to my ears. Thank you spirits. *(Floating around the room.)* Me? Helen of Troy? Venus Di Milo? Cleopatra? Me? *(Looks down at her appearance.)* Oh, I must prepare myself for him. *(Blows another kiss towards the front door.)* Mai tarziu. *('Later'.) [See Authors' Notes.] (Exits French doors.)*

*(***BUD** *enters through the front entrance with wine and chocolates. He stops, seeing no one in the room, as* **ANNIE** *enters from the kitchen.)*

ANNIE. *(Comes down.)* Oh, hello, can I help you?

BUD. Oh, I hope so.

ANNIE. What?

BUD. I have never seen such a vision of loveliness, such beauty, such charm. I have dreamed of love many times in my life, but the face in my dreams was never as beautiful as the one I see before me now.

ANNIE. Ah, you must be Mr. Davis.

BUD. At your service madam. *(He gives a very geriatric bow.)* But, please, call me Bud.

ANNIE. I'm Annie Seville, we talked on the phone.

BUD. Your name is of no importance. I see only the figure before me. The smile, the grace, the unparalleled beauty of a woman.

ANNIE. *(Flustered.)* Oh, thank you. You wouldn't be playing fast and loose with me would you?

BUD. Madam, at my age you have to be loose to be fast, and I am neither. But believe me when I say, you have the face that launched a thousand ships, Helen of

Troy, the body of the Venus de Milo, and clearly the mind and spirit of Cleopatra.

ANNIE. Mr. Davis, you are good.

BUD. *(Hands* ANNIE *the wine and chocolates, which she puts on the end table.)* Please accept these as a token of my sincerity in our future relationship.

ANNIE. Thank you, Mr. Davis.

BUD. Please, call me Bud.

ANNIE. Alright. Bud would you mind if we had a little chat, there's something I'd like to discuss with you.

BUD. Not at all, I'd love to spend time talking with someone as beautiful as you.

ANNIE. *(Motions for* BUD *to sit on the couch left as she crosses to sit on the couch right.)* Bud, I'd like to make you a very serious offer to purchase Monet Manor.

BUD. Oh, Ms. Seville, for reasons that have little to do with money, I am determined to turn the manor into a retirement home for ladies. And unless the architectural adviser I have hired to conduct a feasibility study, tells me that the conversion cost will be totally prohibitive, that is what I intend to do. Of course, if you would like to stay, I will be more than happy to reserve you a room.

ANNIE. I see, well, in that case, there is something about the manor, you don't know, that I feel obligated to tell you. It's haunted.

(BUD laughs as GEORGE enters from up left.)

Hi Dad, come meet Mr. Davis, I was just telling him about our resident ghost.

GEORGE. *(Shakes hands with* BUD.) Hello, Mr. Davis, I'm George.

BUD. Hello, please call me Bud. Surely you two don't believe all that malarkey about ghosts?

ANNIE. But Dad and I have both seen the ghost, haven't we Dad?

GEORGE. What Annie says is true, I've seen her.

BUD. Her?

ANNIE. Dad, why don't you show Mr. Davis his room.

GEORGE. *(Stands and moves upstage to bedroom two.)* Right, good idea.

(**BUD** *stands, goes and picks up his luggage and follows* **GEORGE**.)

Here, let me. *(Takes* **BUD***'s suitcase from him as he opens the door.)* It's small, but comfortable. *(Sets the suitcase inside the room.)*

BUD. *(Peeks in.)* You're sure it was a female ghost?

ANNIE. Mr. Davis, I hope you don't mind, but I have arranged to have a séance this evening, conducted by the Contesa Marilena de Buzau Si Severin, our neighbor. She is a well known psychic, who is convinced there are spirits in this house. We'd like you to attend so you can see for yourself.

BUD. *(Moves downstage towards* **ANNIE** *and stands behind the chair.)* I don't believe a word of it, but as I met the Contesa earlier, and if you, and a female ghost are going to be present, count me in.

GEORGE. *(Closes the door and moves downstage.)* I'll be there too.

BUD. I'd also like my adviser, Mr. Oppenheimer to be in attendance if that's alright. That way we can have an impartial eye witness. Not that I believe they'll be anything to see.

GEORGE. Ah but you haven't seen this ghost Mr. Davis.

ANNIE. *(Gives* **GEORGE** *"a look".)* I have no problem with Mr. Oppenheimer attending.

(They hear a car outside.)

BUD. That's probably him now, I'll just go and see. *(Exits front entrance.)*

ANNIE. Boy, he's quite a character.

GEORGE. *(Sits in the chair.)* Talking of characters did I ever tell you the story of the two hunters?

ANNIE. No Dad, but I'm sure I'm about to hear it.

GEORGE. Well, there are these two hunters out in the woods and one of them seems to have a heart attack and collapses on the ground. The other guy doesn't know what to do, so he whips out his cell phone and calls 911. He describes what happened to the operator, and tells her he thinks the guy is dead. Then he asks: what should I do? The operator immediately responds: The first thing we need to do is make absolutely certain he's dead. The guy says, OK, hold on a minute, there's a pause and then the operator hears a gun shot. The guy comes back on the phone and says, OK. He's definitely dead. Now what?

ANNIE. *(Long pause.)* …OK., go on.

GEORGE. What do you mean go on?

ANNIE. You didn't say what happened next.

GEORGE. Nothing happened next… He's dead. You don't get it do you?

ANNIE. How am I supposed to get a joke if you only tell half of it?

GEORGE. Annie, I… Oh never mind. I'm going to go lie down, I feel a shin splint coming on, must be from going up and down those damp, basement stairs. *(Exits up left.)*

(Enter **BUD** *followed by* **BERNARD OPPENHEIMER** *carrying a suitcase in one hand and his cell phone in the other.* **BERNARD** *puts his suitcase down, just inside the front entrance. They move towards* **ANNIE**.*)*

*(***BERNARD***, age 30+, is a freelance property appraiser and architectural adviser, hired by* **BUD** *to do a cost analysis on the feasibility of turning Monet Manor into a retirement home for women. He is overtly motivated with financial matters, to the point of appearing very mercenary. He has an obsession with his cell phone as he is constantly answering calls at all times. He is wearing a button down shirt, tie, and khaki pants.)*

BUD. Annie I'd like you to meet Mr. Oppenheimer, my architectural adviser.

ANNIE. *(Stands.)* Pleased to meet you.

(**ANNIE** *reaches out to shake hands, but, just as she does,* **BERNARD** *'s cell phone begins to ring.)*

BERNARD. *(Nods to* **ANNIE** *as he answers the phone.)* Hello, B.O. here.

(He moves slightly up stage to finish the call as **ANNIE** *looks at* **BUD** *and starts to laugh.)*

Right, well, watch that situation closely, and call me if there's a change. *(Hangs up and moves toward* **ANNIE***.)* Sorry about that, please call me…

(His cell phone rings again, he looks at it and answers.)

Hello, B.O. here. *(Moves slightly up stage.)* OK. I'll call you back later. *(Hangs up and moves toward* **ANNIE***.)* Hello An…

(His cell phone rings again, he looks at it.)

Excuse me, important. *(Moves upstage.)* Hello, B.O. here.

ANNIE. *(To* **BUD***.)* Why don't you introduce me to Mr. B.O. later, I'll just make sure his room is ready *(Exits up left, taking the wine and chocolates with her.)*

(**BERNARD** *hangs up his phone.)*

BUD. Really Bernie, don't you think…

BERNARD. It's Bernard *(He pronounces his name the French way, "Bearnard".)*

BUD. Right. OK Bearnard, *(He over accentuates the name.)* Ms. Seville is a beautiful woman, if you haven't noticed, and beautiful women do not deserve to be ignored.

BERNARD. Ah yes, I forgot. You and women. I am sorry about the calls Mr. Davis and I do agree with you that it was wrong of me not to pay more attention to the lovely Ms. Seville. However, they were important calls. I will try to correct that later when we meet again.

(His phone rings.)

Excuse me please.

BUD. Here we go again…

BERNARD. Hello, B.O. here. I'm in a meeting, if it's an emergency, text me. *(Quickly hangs up.)* OK, we shouldn't be disturbed.

BUD. I hope not. Remember, I'm paying you a big fat fee to find out what it will cost to turn this place into a women's retirement home. Not to answer your phone.

BERNARD. Mr. Davis, I may be expensive, but I can assure you that you will find my work very thorough. *(Looks around.)* Are you quite sure you want to go through with this? This house is quite old, and the cost to bring a place like this up to code, not to mention the design aspect, could become quite costly.

BUD. You just do your job, and find out how many chicks can stay here. Don't you concern yourself with the money.

BERNARD. *(He takes out of his pocket a small appliance which looks exactly like a stud finder, complete with flashing lights. He then places it on the wall left, by the table, and slides it around.)* Mr. Davis, where money is involved, I'm always concerned.

BUD. What is that? What are you doing?

BERNARD. It's an electro-magnetic field transducer.

BUD. A what?

BERNARD. It's like a stud finder but it locates electrical wiring in the walls. This little machine will save you many hours of my time. In layman's terms it locates live wires.

BUD. Really? I'm impressed. Just keep it away from me, I'll have it lighting up like Coney Island. Oh by the way, I almost forgot, I need you to come to the séance tonight.

BERNARD. The what?

BUD. The séance.

BERNARD. I wouldn't be caught dead at a séance.

BUD. Very funny Bernie.

BERNARD. *(Reacts to the **BERNIE**.)* It's Bernard.

BUD. *(Ignores **BERNARD**'s reaction.)* Listen, supposedly the place is haunted, and they're holding a séance to see if anything happens. I want you there as an impartial witness.

BERNARD. That will cost you extra, it wasn't in our original contract.

BUD. How much extra?

BERNARD. Do I have to turn off my phone?

BUD. I'm not sure, but I think so.

BERNARD. Then the price just went up. Two hundred dollars.

BUD. That's outrageous Bernie.

BERNARD. It's Bernard and take it or leave it.

BUD. I'll take it I suppose. Just make sure you're there.

BERNARD. I'll be there, but for the record, I don't believe in ghosts, do you?

BUD. Of course not, but Ms. Seville and her dad both seem pretty convinced.

ANNIE. *(Enters up left.)* Your room is all ready Mr. Oppenheimer.

BERNARD. Right, thank you. I'll see you later Mr. Davis.

*(He picks up his suitcase and moves up left as **BUD** crosses right and sits on the couch right side.)*

Please call me Bernard. I really must apologize for my rudeness earlier,…

(His phone rings and he tries ignore it.)

It's just that…

(His phone continues to ring as he again tries to ignore it, but it's obvious he is struggling.)

Well…uh

ANNIE. Yes?

BERNARD. *(Phone still ringing.)* It's just that, I'm sorry.

(Phone rings again and he quickly answers.)

Hello, B.O. here.

(Smiles apologetically as **ANNIE** *exits up left followed by* **BERNARD***.)*

(Enter **MARILENA** *through the French Doors. She is now dressed in a short evening gown, preferably with sequins, and dress shoes. She is wearing a tiara, and looking every bit the Romanian Contesa. She sweeps into the room and waltzes around, as* **BUD** *stands and stares at her every movement. He then moves to join her in the waltz and they meet center stage and join hands with her right hand up and his left hand up. Then* **BUD** *becomes totally rigid.)*

BUD. *(Groans.)* Aaarrgh!

MARILENA. What?

BUD. My back.

MARILENA. Here, let me help you.

(She guides him as he shuffles backwards, still in a totally rigid position with his arm up, to the front center of the couch. He is facing down left. She gently presses on his shoulders to get him to sit, but it doesn't work. She then pulls on the waistband of his pants to get him to sit. As she does his pants slide down revealing boxer shorts with bright red hearts all over them. His right arm remains above his head and his right leg remains rigid as his left leg bends. He sits on the couch as his right leg goes between her legs. As she tries to remove herself, she ends up falling on top of him.)

(Enter **ANNIE** *from up left. She immediately sees them and moves down stage behind the couch.* **BUD** *gives* **ANNIE** *a finger wave.)*

ANNIE. Mr. Davis, I realize this is now your house, but do you have to carry on in the living room with *(She stops* *and looks closely at the woman.)* Marilena? I don't believe it. *(She wheels around and exits up left.)*

(BUD *and* **MARILENA** *struggle to their feet as* **BUD** *pulls up his pants.)*

BUD. Oh, whatever you did, and I might say I enjoyed it, my back is better. You have a gift, thank you my Cherie.

(BUD *kisses her hand.)*

MARILENA. I really did nothing.

BUD. And speaking of gifts, I shall return immediately with your French wine and Swiss chocolates. *(Exits front entrance.)*

GEORGE. *(Enters from up left, sees* **MARILENA** *and stops and stares.)* Marilena, is that you? Oh my goodness… I never…you look so different.

MARILENA. *Sunt inca eu ('I am still me'.) [See Authors' Notes.]*

GEORGE. I wish you came with English sub-titles. Annie never told me I had to dress up for the séance.

MARILENA. George, you don't have to dress up, but sometimes it helps.

GEORGE. Good, because I'm really comfortable as I am. I'll see you later then. *(Exits up left.)*

BUD. *(Enters from the front entrance with wine and chocolates.)* For you my love, gifts for a goddess. *(Hands her the gifts.)*

MARILENA. How kind, but I cannot possibly…wait, I feel the spirits, they are speaking.

BUD. *(Looks around.)* Can you tell them to speak up? I'm a little hard of hearing.

MARILENA. They are telling me to follow my heart.

BUD. Then, you will meet with me?

MARILENA. Spirits? *(Pauses.)* Yes, oh yes.

BUD. Your house?

MARILENA. I have guests, it is not possible.

BUD. I would suggest my room, and although I am rather athletic, there is only one tiny little bed. Is there somewhere else here that would work?

MARILENA. This is all very exciting, but…maybe…no.

BUD. What? What?

MARILENA. There is a room that is not being used. *(Pauses, as if listening to the spirits.)*

BUD. Are the spirits still talking? Are they telling you where the room is?

MARILENA. No, I know where it is, what I'm asking them is should I tell you?

BUD. Well?

MARILENA. Oh my! Answer me spirits… Can I?… Should I?…

(They move right and she opens the bedroom door.)

BUD. *(Follows her to the door and peeks in then looks at his watch.)* Perfect. Shall we rendezvous in twenty minutes?

MARILENA. *Cred ca imi placi. (I think I like you.)* **[See Authors' Notes.]**

BUD. Is that a yes?

*(**MARILENA** nods her head in agreement as **BUD** dances a little jig.)*

In twenty minutes then, please excuse me… I need to… I have to…er, er, get some supplies. *Au revoir* my *chéri. (He exits jauntily to bedroom two.)*

MARILENA. *(Excitedly whirls around.)* Twenty minutes to heaven.

CHARMAINE. *(Enters from bedroom one.)* Howdy Contesa, ya'll look as happy as a pig in… *(Stops and giggles.)* …Well you know.

MARILENA. *(Stops twirling.)* Good afternoon Ms. Beauregard.

CHARMAINE. *(Moves down stage.)* Why you're sparkling like sunshine on a spring morning…any special reason?

MARILENA. Yes, yes, oh yes, the stars are in place, the planets are aligned, the spirits are calling me. I think I have found my true love.

CHARMAINE. Well if that don't put sugar in the julip!

GEORGE. *(Enters from up left.)* Marilena, are you still here?

MARILENA. I was just leaving, excuse me please. *(Exits with a flourish through the French doors.)*

CHARMAINE. Well hello there Georgie Porgie…long time no see. Where have you been hiding?

GEORGE. *(Comes down.)* I…I…I haven't been hiding. I had work to do…important work.

CHARMAINE. *(Puts her arms around his neck.)* Why I've been ever so lonely. Why don't we just slip through the bookcase into my room.

GEORGE. *(Gently disengages and backs away right.)* In the middle of the afternoon?

CHARMAINE. *(Pursues him right.)* Well it's evenin' somewhere.

GEORGE. *(Backing right toward the bedroom door.)* Where?

CHARMAINE. Somewhere.

*(**GEORGE** is now backed up against the bedroom door. **CHARMAINE** reaches around him, opens the door and pushes him in.)*

Here.

(Leaving the bedroom door open, she pushes him onto the bed, falls on top of him and smothers him with kisses.)

*(**BERNARD** enters from up left with his tape measure in one hand, his cell phone in his pants pocket, a notepad in his shirt pocket and a pencil behind his ear. He moves right on the landing, comes down, moves towards the bedroom door measuring the entire distance recording the measurements in the notebook. Just outside the bedroom door his cell phone rings.)*

BERNARD. Hello, B.O. here.

(**CHARMAINE** *and* **GEORGE** *sit bolt upright and listen.*)

Yes of course. If it goes up, hold on to it. If it goes down, let it go.

(**GEORGE** *and* **CHARMAINE** *look at each other and mouth the words "hold on to it" and "let it go".*)

I agree, protecting our assets is important.

(**GEORGE** *places his hands over his crotch and nods vigorously, while* **CHARMAINE** *giggles.*)

We definitely need to be in a position to take advantage of any upward movement.

(**CHARMAINE** *pushes* **GEORGE** *onto his back and straddles him.*)

GEORGE. (*Rolls* **CHARMAINE** *off him and stands up.*) Wait a minute, who is that?

ANNIE. (*Enters from up left.*) Hello Mr. Oppenheimer. (*She moves right and comes down towards* **BERNARD**.) Can I help you?

BERNARD. Gotta go. (*Clicks off his phone and puts it in his back pants pocket.*)

GEORGE. (*Stops dead in his tracks and motions to* **CHARMAINE** *to get off the bed.*) It's Annie, quick, hide. She can't find us in here. I'll never hear the end of it. (*He looks frantically around.*) Yes, the bathroom

(**GEORGE** *opens the bathroom door,* **CHARMAINE** *exits and* **GEORGE** *follows closing the door.*)

BERNARD. Oh, hello Ms. Seville.

ANNIE. Why don't you call me Annie?

BERNARD. Of course Annie, then I am Bernard.

ANNIE. OK Bernard. (*Taking her cue from him, she pronounces it his way "Bearnard".*) Is there anything I can do for you?

BERNARD. I was just measuring and wondered about this room here.

ANNIE. Oh, it used to be a study, but we turned it into a small bedroom for Mrs. Hammond, the previous owner of Monet Manor,

BERNARD. Well, if you could just hold the end of the tape measure for me that would be helpful. *[See Authors' Notes.]*

(He hands her one end of the tape.)

From the door I think. *(He measures the back wall, then writes down measurement in the notebook and puts it back in his shirt pocket.)* Now perhaps that one.

(He indicates the down stage wall. As he measures the bathroom wall with his back to **ANNIE**, *she moves to the down right corner as he turns to his right facing upstage. The tape is now wrapped around him. He is immediately above the bed, as* **ANNIE** *with her back to him reaches with her end of the tape for the down right corner of the room. This tightens the tape and pulls* **BERNARD** *backward onto the bed. As he falls he pulls on his end of the tape and* **ANNIE** *falls on top of him. They move and become further entangled as* **BERNARD***'s cell phone rings.* **BERNARD** *tries to reach his phone but is not able to do so as, by now, they are hopelessly tangled up together.)*

BERNARD. *(cont.)* Can you get it?

ANNIE. *(Manages to get the phone, and tries to hand it to* **BERNARD***, but his hands are all caught up in the tape, so she answers.)* Hello. *(She turns to face* **BERNARD***.)* It's for you.

BERNARD. No kidding! So, answer it.

ANNIE. Mr. Oppenheimer's line. You've never heard of him? OK, how about Bernard. No? OK, this is B.O. Well I'm not B.O. obviously. You want B.O. Well alright, I have B.O. No I don't. I mean… Can I get you B.O.? Well, he's a little tied up at the moment, can I take a message? Tell him what? *(Turns to* **BERNARD***.)* You're supposed to stop whatever you're doing, take immediate action, and take matters into your own hands.

(**GEORGE** *quietly opens the bathroom door, sticks his head out and listens.*)

BERNARD. Really?

ANNIE. Really.

(**BERNARD** *grabs* **ANNIE**.)

ANNIE. Mr. Oppenheimer, what do you think you're doing?

BERNARD. Following your instructions.

(**GEORGE** *returns to the bathroom leaving the door open just a crack.*)

ANNIE. Those weren't my instructions they were his. *(Shows him the phone.)*

BERNARD. Well they were fun don't you think?

(**ANNIE** *gives him 'a look'.*)

I'm sorry, tell him I'll call him back.

ANNIE. He'll call you back, *(Hangs up the phone.)*

(**GEORGE** *and* **CHARMAINE** *enter from the bathroom holding a super sized bath towel covering their entire bodies from the knees up. They shuffle left out of the bedroom into the living room watched by* **ANNIE** *and* **BERNARD**.)

Dad, I'd know your legs anywhere. And whose are those other legs? What's going on?

(**BERNARD** *now sitting up, is disentangling himself from the tape measure and accidentally pulls them both down again. Eventually they manage to sit up free of the tape.*)

CHARMAINE. *(Now outside the bedroom door.)* Why Georgie you're ever so clever. Now, you get rid of those two, and just give me ten minutes to slip into something more comfortable, and I'll meet you back here. I promise you there'll be more fireworks than the Fourth of July. *(Sweeps off and exits to bedroom one.)*

GEORGE. *(Returns to the bedroom with a grin on his face.)* Annie, who is this guy? More importantly, does he measure up to your expectations?

ANNIE. Very funny Dad. Dad, this is B.O.

(**GEORGE** *frowns and* **BERNARD** *looks at her.*)

I'm sorry. Dad this is Mr. Oppenheimer, he is Mr. Davis's architectural adviser. This is my dad, George.

GEORGE. Nice to meet you Mr. Oppenheimer.

(**GEORGE** *and* **BERNARD** *shake hands.*)

(*To* **ANNIE,** *now laughing.*) And what advice is he giving you Annie?

ANNIE. You're just a riot Dad.

BERNARD. Please call me Bernard.

(*His phone rings and* **ANNIE** *hands him his phone.*)

Excuse me *(He moves into the living room.)* Hello B.O. here.

(**GEORGE** *looks at* **ANNIE** *questioningly.*)

ANNIE. Don't worry Dad that's just B.O.'s M.O.

GEORGE. Annie, just what is going on here?

ANNIE. I was about to ask you the same thing. Who was that behind the towel with you? And what were you doing in the bathroom?

GEORGE. Have I ever told you, you ask too many questions. My lumbago is killing me and all you can do is stand here and give me the Spanish Inquisition. And please notice that I did not ask you what you were doing on the bed with Mr. B.O.

BERNARD. It's Bernard.

ANNIE. We were not doing anything. I was just trying to help him measure the room.

BERNARD. *(Hangs up his phone and sticks his head in the bedroom door.)* If it's alright with you Annie, could you show me the rest of the house? I will have to see every room in order to figure out what can and cannot be converted into small private suites.

GEORGE. Even the basement?

BERNARD. Especially the basement. I need to examine it carefully for the structural integrity of all the walls, and all the electrical circuits.

*(**GEORGE** and **ANNIE** look at each other.)*

GEORGE *(Whispers to **ANNIE**.)* It's OK, it's all cleaned up. He won't find anything.

ANNIE. Good. *(Comes into the living room.)* Bernard, I'd be happy to show you the house. The basement stairs are off the kitchen. *(She opens the kitchen door.)* The basement door is that one just to the left of the fridge. Will you be alright alone?

BERNARD. Yes, thank you. *(Exits to the kitchen.)*

ANNIE. *(To **GEORGE** who has joined her in the living room.)* Dad, are you sure it's OK for him to be in the basement?

GEORGE. Quite sure. You've seen it a thousand times, the brick wall looks like a brick wall, and he'll never find the switch that opens it, not in a million years.

ANNIE. *(Sits on the couch left side.)* Alright, if you say so, but I've got a bad feeling that something is going to go wrong.

GEORGE. *(Sits on the chair.)* You sound just like Murphy.

ANNIE. Who's Murphy?

GEORGE. You know, Murphy's Law?

ANNIE. Oh, right, I think I do, just remind me.

GEORGE. Murphy's Law states that if anything can go wrong it will.

ANNIE. Thanks Dad.

GEORGE. But do you know O'Toole's addendum to Murphy's Law?

ANNIE. *(Pauses and looks at **GEORGE**.)* Is this another one of your jokes?

GEORGE. Well yes, kind of.

ANNIE. What do you mean kind of? It's either a joke or it's not.

GEORGE. Then it's a joke.

ANNIE. OK, who's O'Toole.

GEORGE. I don't know who O'Toole was, any more than I know who Murphy was.

ANNIE. Alright Dad, tell your joke.

GEORGE. You know that Murphy's Law states that if anything can go wrong it will. Well, O'Toole's addendum states that Murphy was an optimist.

(ANNIE pauses and looks at him.)

You don't get it do you.

ANNIE. Yes I do, I just don't think it's funny.

GEORGE. *(Stands.)* Oh, never mind. Maybe someday you'll get one of my jokes, hopefully before I'm dead and buried. I'm going to go lie down for awhile, my shin splints are killing me. *(Exits upstage left.)*

(ANNIE lies down on the couch as BUD enters from bedroom two wearing a silk robe with an ascot. He doesn't see ANNIE as he moves towards the downstage bedroom singing. He is just about to enter the bedroom when ANNIE pops her head up.)

ANNIE. Hello Mr. Davis, can I help you?

BUD. *(Startled.)* Um…well I…ah…well…

ANNIE. *(Sits up.)* I'm sorry, I didn't mean to startle you, are you looking for Mr. Oppenheimer?

BUD. Mr. Oppenheimer? *(Looks around.)* Yes, that's right I'm looking for Mr. Oppenheimer, have you seen him?

ANNIE. The last time I saw him, he was going to the basement to do some measuring, I'm sure he'll be back up soon. Do you want me to go get him for you?

BUD. No, no, that's alright. Are you going to be staying here in the living room?

ANNIE. I was just putting my feet up for a little while.

BUD. Oh I see. *(Looks at his watch and then at the bedroom door.)* What time is that séance again?

ANNIE. I'm not sure, whenever Marilena decides I suppose. I'm glad to see you are still planning on being there.

I just want you to know what you're getting into if you do decide to go through with turning this place into a retirement home for women. We really do have a ghost, I just hope you won't be too frightened by her. She has a wicked temper when she gets angry. I sometimes wonder if it isn't because of some guy. You know the old saying, "Hell hath no fury like a woman scorned."

BUD. Believe me Annie, there isn't a woman alive, or dead for that matter, that I can't charm, so don't you worry about me. This place is looking like it will be just perfect for what I have in mind. *(Looks towards the French doors.)*

ANNIE. Are you sure I can't go and find Mr. Oppenheimer for you? I can't imagine what is taking him so long.

BUD. No, no, there's no hurry, I'll just go back to my room and wait for her – I mean him. *(Exits to bedroom two.)*

*(**ANNIE** lies down again, and closes her eyes as **MARILENA** enters through the French doors. She is now dressed in a raincoat, head scarf and carrying a basket filled with rose petals. She moves somewhat furtively towards the bedroom door. Half way across the room she sees **ANNIE**, stops dead in her tracks, then starts to walk slowly backward, hoping to escape.)*

ANNIE. *(Opens her eyes.)* Hello Marilena. Can I do something for you? *(Stands up.)*

MARILENA. Er – er – no not really. I just came over to check out the vibrations, you know, before the séance. *(Starts to sway around the room.)*

ANNIE. Well, how are they?

MARILENA. Oh fine, just fine.

ANNIE. Is it raining?

MARILENA. No, *(Looks at her own raincoat.)* but it looks like it. Are you going to stay here in the living room?

ANNIE. Why does everybody want to know what I'm doing in the living room? Actually, I was going to take a nap, but it doesn't look like it's going to happen. Now that you've checked the vibrations, shouldn't you be going home and getting ready for tonight?

MARILENA. I suppose so.

ANNIE. As it doesn't look like I'm going to get any rest, I might as well get some fresh air. Come on, I'll keep you company through the garden.

(They exit through the French doors.)

(The kitchen door opens slowly and **BERNARD** *enters furtively. He is carrying* **ANNIE***'s sorority bag with the letters Delta Mu clearly visible. He looks around, sees no one, closes the kitchen door and heads up left. He has gone only a step or two when he sees* **ANNIE** *re-enter through the French doors.* **BERNARD** *quickly shuffles backwards with the bag behind his back into bedroom and quickly hides the bag under the bed.)*

*(***ANNIE** *looks around and heads towards the couch.)* Good, no one's around, maybe now I can get some rest. *(Lies down with her head stage right and closes her eyes.)*

BERNARD. *(Enters from the bedroom, and sees* **ANNIE***.)* Hello Annie.

ANNIE. *(Startled.)* What? Oh, hi, everything check out all right in the basement? *(Sits up.)*

BERNARD. Oh, you could say that, but I'll probably have to go back down there again.

*(***ANNIE** *yawns.)*

Feeling tired?

ANNIE. A little, *(Yawns again.)* since you still need to measure my room, I think I'll just go lie on the bed in there for a few minutes, as I don't seem to be able to nap out here.

(Starts to move towards the bedroom when **BERNARD** *grabs her and starts to try to dance the tango with her.)*

Whatever are you doing?

BERNARD. Well I heard that instead of a cat nap, the best thing to do to revive yourself is get a little exercise. Just thought I'd help you out.

(Moving her away from the bedroom.)

As a matter of fact, if you've got some time, I could use a little bit of help myself.

ANNIE. Well it doesn't look like I'm going to get my nap, so sure, what do you need?

BERNARD. Can you show me the east side of the house?

*(***GEORGE*** enters from upstage left.)*

ANNIE. Alright, follow me. *(Exits upstage left.)* Hi Dad, I'm just going to help Bernard measure some more rooms.

BERNARD. *(Looks back at the bedroom and then follows* **ANNIE***, as his phone rings.)* Hello B.O. here.

GEORGE. *(Watches them go and gives a little finger wave.)* Good, it looks like that should keep them busy for a while. *(He looks at his watch and moves quickly up to bedroom one. He knocks, opens it a little and calls in.)* Your Georgie Porgie will be waiting for you.

*(***GEORGE*** closes the door, does a little jig downstage to the bedroom door, then enters leaving the door slightly ajar. He stops and does a few muscle poses, with the last one indicating he has strained his back. He then moves into the bathroom where he begins to hum a few bars of Ravel's Bolero as he begins to take his clothes off. Although the audience cannot see him, they see a shoe, another shoe, socks, a shirt, and pants fly out the bathroom door into the room.* **GEORGE** *finally makes an entrance wearing yellow smiley face boxers and a t-shirt. He gets up on the bed, does another muscle pose and crawls underneath the covers, downstage side, pulling them over his head.)*

(Enter **MARILENA** *through the French doors. Still dressed in the raincoat and scarf, carrying the basket, she crosses to the bedroom, closes the door behind her, and takes*

off her raincoat, and drops it in the floor, revealing a sensuous negligee. She sees the figure in the bed and blows kisses while sprinkling the bed with petals. Swirling around the room, she takes off the scarf and waves it around imitating the dance of the seven veils. Finally, she gets into bed upstage side, pulling the covers over her head. There is some movement under the bed clothes.)

MARILENA.	GEORGE.
Oh Bud!	Oh Charmaine!

*(All movement now stops, there is a long pause, then, simultaneously, they both sit up and scream. **GEORGE** is now wearing the scarf over his head.)*

MARILENA. *(Jumps out of bed, grabs her scarf, and picks up her raincoat holding it in front of her like a shield.)* You…how can this be…oh, spirits, what have I done… *(She quickly runs out of the bedroom and exits through the French doors.)*

GEORGE. Marilena? *(Puts on his pants, and picks up his socks and shoes.)* Was that really Marilena? What in heaven's name was she doing here? I mean, I know what she was doing here, but why was she doing it here? *(Pauses and notices the rose petals.)* Well whatever is going on, Marilena certainly helped set the right mood, the only thing missing here is wine. *(Glances at his watch and then exits to the kitchen.)*

*(Enter **BUD** from room two, now dressed in a fancy robe with a scarf around his neck, carrying a bottle of wine and two glasses. With a great flourish, he tangos his way downstage and enters the bedroom. He pours two glasses of wine and sets one on each of the bedside tables. Then he reaches into his robe pocket, takes out a pill bottle, and pops a little blue pill. Finally, he takes off his robe revealing boxers with hearts all over them. He hops into bed downstage side, pulling the covers up over his head.)*

*(Enter **CHARMAINE** from bedroom one, now wearing an attractive robe and carrying her sorority bag with Delta Mu clearly visible. She looks furtively around,*

then quickly tip toes to the bedroom and enters, closing the door. She takes a glass of wine from the side table with her, and enters the bathroom closing the door. Hearing the door close, **BUD** *pokes his head out. He watches as the bathroom door opens slightly and we hear the humming of the 'strip tease' song and see bra and panties come twirling out.* **BUD** *reacts and again pulls the covers up over his head just as* **CHARMAINE** *enters from the bathroom, still in her robe and carrying the Delta MU bag. She takes out a bottle of perfume, which she sprays around the room. She picks up her clothes and throws everything into her bag and kicks it under the bed, left side. Finally, she gets into bed, upstage side and pulls the covers over her head. There is frantic movement under the covers.)*

CHARMAINE. *(From beneath the covers.)* Why Georgie, you've got me hotter than the proverbial cat on a hot tin roof.

BUD. *(Sits bolt upright.)* Georgie?

CHARMAINE. *(Sits up.)* You!

BUD. Yes of course it's me. Who are you?

CHARMAINE. Who am I? Who am I? You don't remember me?

BUD. No, er yes, er, should I?

CHARMAINE. You were my Budly Studly Do Right, till you done me wrong.

BUD. Done you wrong? Bud the Stud? Done you wrong? Then let me try to do you right.

CHARMAINE. *(Gets out of bed.)* You aren't going to do anything you miserable little weasel.

BUD. Aren't you pleased to see me?

CHARMAINE. You're about as welcome as a skunk at a lawn party.

BUD. Don't be like that. After all, you're here, I'm here, and we have this gorgeous bed…

CHARMAINE. We don't have anything. You lower than a snake's belly varmint, *(She grabs a bag [B.O.'s] from* *under the bed and charges out of the bedroom and exits to bedroom one.)*

BUD. Such a wasted opportunity. Ah well there's still the fair and beautiful Contesa. *(He primps a little, then gets back into bed, downstage side, and pulls the covers over his head.)*

(Enter **GEORGE** *from the kitchen carrying a bottle of wine and two glasses. He quickly crosses to the bedroom, enters and closes the door, he sees the wine and the one glass. He then puts down one glass and puts the wine and the other glass into the bathroom. He returns immediately, takes off his shirt, shoes and pants, and jumps into bed, pulling the covers over his head. In the meantime* **BERNARD** *has entered from up left, crossed right, and furtively entered the bedroom. He bends down, and takes the bag from under the bed. As he straightens up he notices the figures in the bed. There is a movement under the covers when suddenly both* **GEORGE** *and* **BUD** *sit bolt upright, look at each other, look at* **BERNARD**, *look at each other again and scream.)*

BERNARD. Well – well – well! I would never have guessed.

BUD. Guessed what?

BERNARD. Well, you two, you know.

BUD. What do you mean "you two, you know"? Oh, you don't think that him and me – That's ridiculous. Tell him George.

GEORGE. That's ridiculous. Wait a minute, wait a minute, Where did you get that bag?

BERNARD. I'm sure you can tell me. *(He turns and heads up towards the steps.)*

GEORGE. *(Leaps out of bed and follows still in his underwear picking up his pants, shoes and socks.)* Bernard. Hold on.

BERNARD. *(Turns.)* We'll talk later, *(Indicates the bedroom.)* When you're not busy here.

GEORGE. Oh my lord. *(He rushes off into the kitchen carrying his clothes.)*

BUD. *(Now out of bed and still in his underwear follows them into the living room.)* Listen Bernie –

BERNARD. It's Bearnard.

BUD. Whatever! I just don't want you to think that I am – er – well, that George and I – er – you know.

BERNARD. Don't worry, your little secret is safe with me.

BUD. There is no secret you idiot.

BERNARD. Oh I see. I had no idea that you were already out of the closet.

BUD. I'm not out of the closet, I was never in the closet. You don't seem to understand.

BERNARD. I understand perfectly. I consider myself very broadminded, and if I may say so, very understanding of other peoples life styles and I think it would be inappropriate for us to discuss the matter any further. So, if you will excuse me.

(He turns and hurries off up left leaving **BUD** *with his mouth open. He shrugs, returns to the bedroom, picks up his clothes and heads up to his room as* **ANNIE** *enters from up left. They meet just outside* **BUD***'s door.)*

ANNIE. Mr. Davis, I do understand that this Manor belongs to you, but while we are still here I would appreciate it if you could dress a little more appropriately.

BUD. None of my chicks have ever complained about the way I dress before.

ANNIE. Well, I'm not one of your chicks.

BUD. This isn't getting us anywhere.

ANNIE. Good, because we're not going anywhere.

BUD. You know, we can change that. I was just going to my room, perhaps you would care to join me.

ANNIE. Yes. When pigs can fly! Good day Mr. Davis.

*(***BUD** *exits to bedroom two and* **ANNIE** *comes down, sits on the couch right and picks up a magazine. Almost immediately,* **GEORGE**, *now wearing his pants and still carrying his shoes and socks, flings open the kitchen*

door and rushes in breathing heavily, hyper-ventilating, comes down to behind the chair.)

GEORGE. *(Gasping for air.)* Annie, we're in trouble.

ANNIE. Are you alright Dad?

GEORGE. Absolutely not.

ANNIE. What's wrong, come sit down.

GEORGE. There's no time for that. He found it and the money's gone.

ANNIE. Slow down, who found what?

GEORGE. The cell phone maniac. You know – "Hello B.O. here." ...He found the printing press, and the money is missing.

ANNIE. Oh boy, you're right, we're in trouble.

GEORGE. Don't just sit there, do something.

ANNIE. *(Pauses.)* I need you to go and get Bernard in here.

GEORGE. Me? Can't you see my asthma is acting up again, my blood pressure is rising, my head is pounding, and I'm about to have a heart attack. *(Flops into the chair and puts on his shoes and socks.)*

ANNIE. Alright Dad, I'll go get him. *(Exits up left.)*

MARILENA. *(Enters from the French doors. She is wearing the same outfit as in Act I.)* Hellooo. *(Sees* **GEORGE** *in the chair. He waves his hand from the chair and* **MARILENA** *moves right towards him.)* George, I have to talk to you before the séance starts. I must apologize...the bedroom... I am so ashamed. That man, Bud Davis, he got me all confused – he –

GEORGE. *(Stands.)* No, no, I am the one who needs to apologize. I got carried away by Charmaine's attentions and before I knew it, I had made plans for a rendezvous. I'm really not good with all this...this kind of thing.

MARILENA. *(Holds out both hands towards him.)* Nor me George. I don't know what got into me. I feel better now.

GEORGE. *(Takes* **MARILENA**'*s hands.)* Me too.

(Enter **ANNIE** *and* **BERNARD**, *carrying the bag, from up left.* **GEORGE** *and* **MARILENA**, *still holding hands quickly stop, but not before* **ANNIE** *sees them.)*

MARILENA. Well, I must be off and get ready for the séance. See you shortly. Larevedere. *(Exits French doors.)*

ANNIE. Dad, Mr. Oppenheimer says he wants to talk to us.

*(***GEORGE** *sits on the couch right side,* **ANNIE** *on the couch left. side, and* **BERNARD** *sits in the chair.)*

BERNARD. Alright, here it is, plain and simple. I know, that you know, that I know what's going on around here.

GEORGE. What? Why do I always fell like I need an interpreter.

ANNIE. You were right Dad, he knows about the printing press.

GEORGE. What are you going to do?

BERNARD. How would you like a partner?

GEORGE. What?

ANNIE. You're not going to turn us in?

BERNARD. Not if we can make a deal.

GEORGE. What sort of deal?

BERNARD. I was thinking equal partners. Of course, you'd have to teach me how it all works.

GEORGE. Annie, does this mean I wouldn't have to run the press anymore?

ANNIE. I guess not, at least not all the time.

GEORGE. Then I'm all for it. You know, my back feels better already.

BERNARD. We will be just like one happy family.

GEORGE. Talking of families, did I ever tell you the story of the couple who got into an argument driving round the countryside.

ANNIE. Dad! Not another joke.

BERNARD. Why not, I love a good joke.

GEORGE. See Annie. OK here we go. There's this married couple driving round the countryside and they get into a terrible fight. They are passing by a farmyard full of pigs and goats and other animals, and the husband says, "Relatives of yours?" The wife says, "Yes, in-laws."

BERNARD. *(Chuckling.)* That's cute George, I like that.

GEORGE. Annie?

(ANNIE looks blankly at him.)

Oh, never mind.

(BERNARD's phone rings and he reaches for it.)

ANNIE. Don't even think about it.

(BERNARD puts the phone back in his pocket.)

How do we know we can trust you?

BERNARD. All my life I've wanted to make money, this is the opportunity of a lifetime. It seems to me, the two of you have a pretty sweet operation going, and I want in. What you have in the bag here looks very real.

ANNIE. That's because it is real.

BERNARD. I don't understand.

ANNIE. That's last month's counterfeit production, exchanged for real bills in Boston last week.

BERNARD. That's brilliant! *(Unzips the bag on his lap.)* We can double, triple, quadruple production. We can produce tens of thousands of these. *(Reaches into the bag and holds up CHARMAINE's bra.)*

GEORGE. *(Holds his hands out as if cupping breasts.)* Yep, that's Charmaine's.

ANNIE. Dad!

GEORGE. Sorry…but Bernard, where's the money?

BERNARD. I don't understand?

ANNIE. *(Takes the bag and bra from BERNARD.)* This must be Charmaine's bag, but I don't know what you're doing with it. How in heaven's name did they get swapped? Dad, you wouldn't know where this bag came from would you?

GEORGE. Ahh, well,…er…it's a long story, and it doesn't really matter right now. We need to focus on the money and how to get it back.

ANNIE. I think I've got an idea.

BERNARD. Great.

ANNIE. But it doesn't involve you.

BERNARD. Right, well I've got to get some figures ready for Mr. Davis, so if you don't need me, I'll be in my room. *(Moves up left.)* Keep me posted partners. *(Exits.)*

ANNIE. OK Dad, here's the plan. You go into Charmaine's room and swap the bag.

GEORGE. Why me, why not you, she's your friend.

ANNIE. Because –

GEORGE. Because what?

ANNIE. Well, you know, you should be able to distract her while you swap the bags, after all, you two seem to have a thing going.

GEORGE. Not any more, she's way too much woman for me.

ANNIE. I'm glad to hear that Dad, but she doesn't know that, and you have a reason to go into the room.

GEORGE. I guess that makes sense, but if I yell for help, come and rescue me.

ANNIE. You've got it. Off you go. *(Hands him the bag.)*

*(**GEORGE** goes to the door of bedroom one, holding the bag behind his back, and knocks. The door opens and we see a hand grab **GEORGE** by the hair and pull him into the room leaving the door open. **GEORGE** yells as he disappears into the room. The audience should hear lots of **GEORGE** and **CHARMAINE** noises off. A few seconds later **GEORGE**, looking disheveled, appears out of the bookcase still holding the bag, which **ANNIE** reaches for.)*

GEORGE. No, no this is still her bag.

*(**ANNIE** pushes him back into the door of bedroom one. More **GEORGE** and **CHARMAINE** noises off. **GEORGE**,*

*looking even more disheveled, reappears out of the
bookcase holding two bags, closes the bookcase behind
him, and leans on it breathing heavily. He hands one
bag to* ANNIE.)

ANNIE. Well done Dad. You look like you just ran a
marathon, come sit down.

(ANNIE *sits on the couch left side and* GEORGE *in the
chair.* GEORGE *places his bag on the floor by his feet.*)

Let's just make sure it's still all here.

(ANNIE *opens her bag and holds up two handfuls of
money as* BUD *opens the door of bedroom two. He is
about to enter, but stops dead in his tracks when he sees*
ANNIE *taking the money out of the bag.*)

(MARILENA *now dressed in her original outfit, enters
from the French doors, carrying a bag.* BUD *sees her and
quickly steps back into his room closing the door.*)

MARILENA. Helloooo, I'm here for the séance.

(ANNIE *quickly puts the money back in the bag and zips
it up as* MARILENA *crosses downstage.*)

Oh my, the vibrations they are strong. *(Starts to move
around the room.)* Again, money, money, money, I am
sensing a definite presence. I am sure we are going to
make contact tonight.

(*She opens her bag and takes out a colored table cloth
and an electric candle that she places in the center of the
table and puts the bag on the floor.*)

It is important that we make the spirits feel welcome.
Money… I feel a very strong presence, it has something
to do with money.

ANNIE. *(Stands holding the bag.)* Marilena, there will only
be five of us for the séance, Charmaine is not feeling
well. So, we will need to get three more chairs from
the kitchen. Dad, why don't you take this into the
kitchen with you. *(Hands him her bag.)*

MARILENA. Let me help you George.

GEORGE. Thank you.

(Carrying the money bag, GEORGE crosses to the kitchen door and holds it open, then follows MARILENA off, as ANNIE picks up the other bag and crosses to the table. She sets the bag in the middle of the table and begins to move the chairs over, as BUD enters from bedroom two.)

BUD. *(Comes downstage.)* Good evening Annie. Interesting centerpiece for a séance.

ANNIE. Oh, that? That's Charmaine's bag, she must have left it out here by mistake, I'll be returning it to her as soon as I'm done here. *(Grabs the bag off the table and heads towards CHARMAINE's room.)*

BUD. Really Annie, you expect me to believe that?

ANNIE. *(Turns back towards BUD.)* Sure, why not?

BUD. Because I know what's in that bag.

ANNIE. *(Moves downstage towards BUD on his right.)* You do?

BUD. Yes, it is quite appealing.

ANNIE. You've seen it?

BUD. Yep, and what I saw was very revealing.

ANNIE. I'm sure it was very exciting for you, and I'm also sure you've seen more than your fair share.

(BERNARD enters from up left and overhears BUD and ANNIE.)

BUD. Not as much as I'd like, that's why I'm so interested in what's in the bag.

ANNIE. Mr. Davis, I've heard about enough. I have to get ready for the séance. Here, have the bag. I'm sure it will be an uplifting experience for you. *(Hands BUD the bag.)*

BERNARD. *(Rushes down to BUD.)* I couldn't help but overhear, Mr. Davis has no right to your bag.

ANNIE. He already knows what's in it so it doesn't really matter.

(BUD turns to his left to leave and BERNARD takes the bag.)

BERNARD. I'll take that.

BUD. This has nothing to do with you young man. Now give me that bag. *(Clutches the bag.)*

BERNARD. *(Tugs back, pulling BUD a few inches.)* It doesn't belong to you.

(BUD let's go and BERNARD stumbles backwards into the chair holding the bag.)

BUD. *(Crosses to the chair and takes the bag.)* I don't know what weird obsession you have with this bag, but Annie gave it to me and what's in it is mine now. *(He unzips the bag and pulls out CHARMAINE's bra.)* *(To ANNIE.)* What happened to…

ANNIE. Yes?

BUD. You know…

ANNIE. Yes?

BERNARD. *(Laughing.)* Mr. Davis, what do you plan to do with your "possession", maybe you'd like to model it for us.

BUD. *(Puts the bra back into the bag.)* I do not find that funny young man. I'm paying you to measure, not to poke fun at me. I will be back shortly, there's something in my room I need for the séance.

(BUD puts the bag down on the end table, looks at BERNARD, takes a few steps towards bedroom two, then quickly comes back down, picks up the bag and exits to bedroom two.)

BERNARD. You could have told me.

ANNIE. And miss you turning into a crazy man.

(Enter GEORGE from the kitchen carrying two chairs followed by MARILENA carrying one. They leave the door open. GEORGE has lipstick on his face. They set the chairs around the table, leaving the right side open.)

(Crosses to the table.) Marilena, have you met Mr. Oppenheimer? He's Mr. Davis's assistant and will be joining us at the séance.

MARILENA. I'm pleased to meet you Mr. Oppenheimer. *(Shakes hands with* **BERNARD**.*)*

BERNARD. Please, call me Bernard.

(His cell phone rings and he moves to the French doors looking outside.)

Hello, B.O. here.

ANNIE. *(Wipes the lipstick off* **GEORGE***'s face.)* Hard time finding chairs?

GEORGE. Marilena was just explaining to me how the séance was going to work.

MARILENA. And George was telling me the cutest joke about a boy and girl ghost. Have you heard it Annie?

ANNIE. Yes.

MARILENA. It was so funny.

GEORGE. At least someone here appreciates a good joke. Well it looks like we're ready. Where's Mr. Davis?

BERNARD. *(Hangs up and turns into the room.)* He's in his room. He said there was something he needed for the séance.

*(***BUD*** enters from bedroom two and comes down.)*

ANNIE. OK everybody, let's get this show on the road. Marilena, where do you want us to sit?

MARILENA. I'll sit here, perhaps George you'd like to sit next to me. Annie, why don't you sit next to your dad, then Mr. Oppenheimer, and we'll have Mr. Davis sit there.

(They all sit.) **[See Authors' Notes.]**

(As **BUD** *sits, he takes a pair of handcuffs out of his pocket and places them on the table.)*

What are those for?

BUD. I'm going to catch me a ghost.

*(***GEORGE*** and ***ANNIE*** look at each other with horror on their faces.)*

MARILENA. Don't be ridiculous, you can't catch a spirit and in any event, you must respect their world. You must not interfere. We do not want to upset the spirits, strange unpredictable things can happen and we must honor the spirit realm.

BUD. OK, I'll put them away, but I don't believe there's going to be a ghost anyway. *(Puts the handcuffs in his pocket.)*

MARILENA. Mr. Davis, we must all clear our minds of mundane worldly matters. It is important that we are all open-minded to the possibility of a visitor. We are here to meet the spirit that resides in this manor. Please, turn off your cell phone Mr. Oppenheimer, and George, can you turn down the lights.

(GEORGE reaches behind him and turns down the lights.) [See Authors' Notes.]

Please everyone, let's hold hands and remain silent. Remember, do not break the circle. *(She begins to hum and sway for a few seconds.)* O…m, o…m. Oh, spirit, we respectfully ask that you honor us with your presence tonight. *(There is a long pause.)* Quiet, the spirit talks to me… I hear you O' spirit.

BUD. What's it saying? Is it a female?

MARILENA. Shhhh, she is very faint and far away. Please spirit, we wish you no harm, Please commune with us, move among us.

BUD. Is she young or old?

BERNARD. She's dead Bud!

MARILENA. Oh – Oh – Oh, she is coming closer, I feel her presence, she is angry.

BUD. I hope she's not one of my chicks.

BERNARD. She's dead Bud!

BUD. Can you see her? Is she beautiful? What does she look like?

BERNARD. She's dead Bud!

MARILENA. Do not move, she approaches.

*(At this point a silvery chiffon clad figure enters the stage from the auditorium and glides up towards the steps. **[See Authors' Notes.]** BUD stands, takes the handcuffs out of his pocket and moves up towards the figure.)*

ANNIE. DAD!

*(**GEORGE** gets up to intercept **BUD**, quickly followed by **ANNIE**.)*

MARILENA. No-No.

*(She gets up and runs up stage after **GEORGE**, **BUD**, and **ANNIE**.)*

*(**GEORGE** has got his arms round **BUD**'s waist, **ANNIE** is hanging on to **BUD**'s shirt, and as **MARILENA** joins the fray they all four go down in a pile on the floor. They look up in the dim light as the silvery figure disappears silently into the bookcase. Immediately a second silvery chiffon clad figure enters the stage from the auditorium, **[See Authors' Notes.]** glides silently up stage and disappears into the open door of the kitchen watched in silence by everybody.)*

(Curtain.)

ACT II

(The action is continuous.)

(As the curtain rises, **BERNARD** *is the first to move. He runs from the table following the ghost into the kitchen.* **GEORGE**, **MARILENA**, **BUD**, *and* **ANNIE** *disentangle themselves and stand up.* **GEORGE** *moves left to the light switch on the wall and switches on the lights. We see* **BUD***'s hand on* **ANNIE***'s derriere.* **MARILENA** *is sobbing.)*

ANNIE. *(Slaps* **BUD** *face.)* Mr. Davis, keep your hands to yourself.

*(***GEORGE** *quickly moves back and takes* **MARILENA** *in his arms.)*

GEORGE. Are you alright my dear?

MARILENA. *(Pointing at* **BUD** *and almost hysterical.)* You, you disturbed the spirit world. Anything could happen now.

BUD. Anything? You mean that ghosts might come back? That's great! *(Sits on the couch right side.)*

MARILENA. *(Howling.)* You don't understand.

GEORGE. Why don't you come and lie down for a few moments, you're obviously upset.

MARILENA. Thank you, I think I will.

*(***MARILENA** *exits to the bedroom followed by* **GEORGE**, *as* **ANNIE** *moves to the table and starts to fold up the table cloth and puts it in* **MARILENA***'s bag, along with the candle.)*

GEORGE. I'm sure you'll feel better after a little rest, I always do.

(**GEORGE** *pulls back the bedspread and helps* **MARILENA** *onto the bed left side, and gives her a quick kiss on her forehead.*)

GEORGE. *(cont.)* I'll be back the first chance I get. *(Returns to the living room, closing the door.)*

BUD. I think it's time for a little chat you two.

(**ANNIE** *moves right and sits in the chair, carrying* **MARILENA**'s *bag, she sets it on the end table.* **GEORGE** *remains standing.*)

ANNIE. That's probably a good idea. So, do you believe me now about this place being haunted? What do you think you're going to do?

BUD. I don't know. Tell me something, do ghosts wear perfume?

ANNIE. What do you mean?

BUD. I could have sworn I smelled perfume on one of the ghosts.

ANNIE. That's impossible.

GEORGE. Which one, there were two?

BUD. I'm not sure, but two ghosts, tends to make me think there really is something going on here. Two would give this place huge publicity. I could charge a lot of money for the chance to live in a real haunted house. They seemed friendly enough, and one of them sure did smell good.

GEORGE. Annie, there were two ghosts.

ANNIE. I know Dad, I know, I was there. Mr. Davis, I'm a little tired right now, could we talk about this later?

BUD. Certainly, maybe we could arrange for another séance. Where there's two ghosts, maybe there's more.

GEORGE. I certainly hope not. I can't stand the excitement. My pacemaker went wild.

ANNIE. Dad, you don't have a pacemaker.

GEORGE. Well, I'm going to need one if there are any more ghosts.

ANNIE. Oh, come on Dad. Sounds like you could use some rest as well.

(**GEORGE** *pauses and looks at the bedroom.*)

I'm sure Marilena is alright, although I've never seen her quite so upset before. Why don't you just let her sleep.

(**ANNIE** *takes* **GEORGE** *by the hand and they exit upstage left.*)

BUD. *(Watches them leave then looks furtively around. He looks at the bedroom door, stands and moves right towards the bedroom.)* Alone at last, don't you fear my little goddess of the ghosts, your Budly Studly will comfort you. *(Takes out his pill bottle from his pocket.)* I'd have made a great boy scout, always prepared. *(Enters the bedroom and goes into the bathroom and closes the door.)*

(**BERNARD** *enters from the kitchen with the money bag, sees the bag on the end table and comes downstage. He sets the money bag down on the table and picks up* **MARILENA**'s *bag. He hurriedly takes all the money, puts it into* **MARILENA**'s *bag, and zips it up just as* **GEORGE** *enters from up left.* **BERNARD** *quickly puts down* **MARILENA**'s *bag.)*

GEORGE. So partner, interesting evening. What are you doing with that bag?

BERNARD. Er…er… I found it in the kitchen and the back door was open. I thought it would be safer in my room.

GEORGE. The back door was open? Well then, just to be safe, why don't we take it down to the basement and lock it up, I'll show you how the doors work.

(**BERNARD** *picks up the bag without the money and they exit to the kitchen, closing the door.)*

(**BUD** *comes out of the bathroom in t-shirt and boxer shorts. He stands by the bed and starts to lift the bedspread.)*

MARILENA. *(Immediately sits bolt upright in bed.)* You…don't you dare come near me, you…you…defiler of spirits, you disbeliever, you…

(She takes her left elbow and strikes **BUD** *in the crotch, he goes down groaning as* **MARILENA** *storms out of the bedroom, picks up her bag from the end table and exits through the French doors.* **BUD** *gets slowly to his feet, picks up his clothes from the bathroom, and moaning and groaning, staggers up stage and exits to bedroom two.)*

(Enter **BERNARD** *from the kitchen, he rushes over to the end table, looks underneath, looks next to the chair as* **GEORGE** *follows him in and watches.)*

GEORGE. Looking for something?

BERNARD. Yes…er…er…no…nothing important.

GEORGE. Right, well then, I think I'll just check on Marilena. See you later.

*(***GEORGE*** exits to the bedroom. Not seeing* **MARILENA**, *he looks in the bathroom as* **BERNARD** *has another frantic look around the living room, looking behind the cushions.* **GEORGE** *opens the bedroom door and stops as he sees* **BERNARD** *bending down under the chair. As* **BERNARD** *straightens up, he sees* **GEORGE** *and starts to exercise touching his toes as his phone rings.)*

GEORGE. *(cont.) (Moves behind the couch.)* Are you alright?

BERNARD. Just doing my exercises, must keep fit. See you later. *(He jogs off as he answers his phone.)* Hello B.O. here. *(Exits upstage left.)*

GEORGE. What a strange young man.

CHARMAINE. *(Now dressed in street clothes, enters from bedroom one.)* Why, hi there Georgie-Porgie, so how'd you like my performance? *(Comes down the steps.)* Personally, I thought I could have been up for the Oscars. *(Now moving right towards him behind the couch.)*

GEORGE. *(With his back to the audience, looking around for an escape.)* You were good.

CHARMAINE. *(Comes upstage of him and runs her fingers up his shirt.)* Good? Honey lamb, you ain't seen nothing yet and I'm not just whistling Dixie here.

*(Now trapped, leaning backwards over the back of the couch, **CHARMAINE** pushes **GEORGE** with one finger. **GEORGE** falls backwards with his legs wide apart in a V, and **CHARMAINE** falls on top of him and tries to smother him with kisses.)*

GEORGE. Help! What are you doing? Let me up! HELP!

*(Finally **GEORGE** manages to escape and runs left, just outside the French doors.)*

Annie, Annie, help.

*(He exits the French doors followed by **CHARMAINE**. **GEORGE** continues to yell.)*

Annie! Help! Stop! You don't understand. Annie!

ANNIE. *(Enters from up left.)* Dad, where are you? *(Comes down to the French doors and looks out.)*

*(**GEORGE** Enters from the main entrance with **CHARMAINE** right behind him. He sees **ANNIE** and hides behind her.)*

GEORGE. Annie, please, tell her to stop, she won't listen to me. *(Puts his hand on his back.)* I think I've pulled a muscle. I'm too old for this.

CHARMAINE. Ya'll don't have to be afraid of little ol' me Georgie. I guess I do carry on a bit sometimes.

*(**ANNIE** Moves right with **GEORGE** remaining behind her, still indicating back pain.)*

ANNIE. Charmaine, I really do think he wants you to stop, he means it. Dad, tell her why, and you can stop pretending to have back trouble, you're safe now.

GEORGE. *(Stands upright.)* Charmaine, please sit down, I have something to say.

*(**CHARMAINE** sits in the chair, **GEORGE** on the couch and **ANNIE** standing behind the end table.)*

I really do find you most attractive, and I was very flattered by your attentions. But, you see, we're not right for each other, and to be honest, I have recently discovered I have feelings for Marilena.

CHARMAINE. Why that was the most charming rejection I have ever heard. Georgie, my granny always said, when one door closes another one opens. I am sorry if I caused you discomfort. I promise I'll behave myself. I'm happy for you and Marilena.

ANNIE. Me too Dad.

GEORGE. Thank you Charmaine.

CHARMAINE. And I thoroughly enjoyed my role as a ghost.

ANNIE. Charmaine, you were totally believable, but did you know there was another ghost?

CHARMAINE. What?

ANNIE. After you left, a second ghost appeared and left through the kitchen.

CHARMAINE. Well if that don't put pepper in the gumbo. Your place really is haunted.

MARILENA. *(Enters from the French doors, carrying her bag and an open umbrella.)* Hellooo.

(MARILENA moves down stage spinning with her open umbrella and the bag, almost running into ANNIE.)

ANNIE. Hi Marilena. What happened? You're certainly in a different mood.

(MARILENA stops spinning, places the bag on the table, closes the umbrella and puts it on the table, and then unzips the bag, reaches in, and holds up a handful of money in each hand.)

MARILENA. This happened.

CHARMAINE. Why shut my mouth, that's enough money to burn a wet mule.

GEORGE. *(Crosses left and looks in the bag.)* Where did you get all this?

MARILENA. The spirits. They rewarded me for preserving the sanctity of their world. They materialized this whole bag of money and left it for me.

ANNIE. *(Crosses to the bag and peeks in.)* It looks about the right amount. Dad, are you thinking what I am?

GEORGE. Right, excuse me a moment. *(Exits to the kitchen.)*

CHARMAINE. *(Gets up and peeks in the bag and pulls out a handful.)* Oh my stars and garters. Why I've never seen so much money. That must have been one rich ghost.

(MARILENA takes her closed umbrella, and holding it like a baton, dances around the room humming "I've Got The Money". She moves up the stairs and twirls just as BUD opens the door of bedroom two, unseen by MARILENA. In one of her movements, she jabs one end of the umbrella into BUD's crotch and he goes down with a loud moan. MARILENA is unaware of what she has just done, while CHARMAINE, and ANNIE watch BUD crawl back into his room and close the door.)

ANNIE. Marilena, I can see how excited you are, but could you please come and sit down before you do anymore damage? Charmaine, please have a seat.

(MARILENA floats down to the couch and sits right as ANNIE takes another peak into the bag.)

CHARMAINE. *(Crosses right and sits on the couch, left.)* I didn't know spirits could materialize things.

MARILENA. I've never experienced it before but I have read about it. It can happen.

CHARMAINE. I'm sure you're right.

(Now dressed in shirt sleeves and a tie, BERNARD enters from up left with papers in his hand. He is about to knock on the door of bedroom two when he sees MARILENA's bag on the table. He peers over the railing.)

BERNARD. Where did you get that bag?

ANNIE. *(Holds up MARILENA's bag.)* You mean this one?

BERNARD. Yes, of course that one.

MARILENA. Oh, that's my bag and it's full of money! The spirits rewarded me. They materialized all that money just for me. *(Pauses.)* No, wait a minute, George, you and Annie helped too. That's why the money was left here and in my bag. I think they meant it for all of us.

BERNARD. No, that can't be possible.

MARILENA. Of course it is, otherwise how would the money have got into my bag?

BERNARD. Ah, well, you see…er…er?

    (He notices **ANNIE** *looking curiously at him.)*

There must be another explanation. That's just not possible.

CHARMAINE. Marilena says it is possible.

ANNIE. Do you have a better explanation Bernard?

BERNARD. Well…er…er… I… I don't know.

ANNIE. *(Looking straight at* **BERNARD**.*)* I think perhaps we should discuss this later. Don't you have a meeting with Mr. Davis?

BERNARD. Yes, and I don't think he's going to like the numbers.

ANNIE. That would be good. *(Crosses right and sits in the chair.)*

BERNARD. Right, I'll see you later than. *(Knocks on Bud's door and exits into bedroom two.)*

GEORGE. *(Enters from the kitchen and hurries over to* **ANNIE** *and whispers.)* The money is not in the basement.

CHARMAINE. *(To* **MARILENA**.*)* What are you going to do with all the money?

MARILENA. I haven't really had time to think about it. Perhaps a new kitchen,…or maybe a new car…or travel…anyway I must be going, I just wanted to share the good news. *(Stands and moves left towards the table and the money.)*

GEORGE. *(Follows her left.)* Marilena my dear. I wouldn't feel comfortable with you all alone in your house with all that money, it isn't safe. How about I lock it up for you till tomorrow. I promise it will be safe in our basement.

MARILENA. Thank you George, that's so sweet of you to care. You're such an honest man, I trust you implicitly. *(Kisses him on the cheek, and picks up the umbrella.) La revedere. (Floats out the French doors.)*

ANNIE. Dad, you can't let her have that money, we need it for the house.

GEORGE. *(Moves right towards* **ANNIE** *holding* **MARILENA**'*s bag.)* Shhh. *(Nodding towards* **CHARMAINE**.*)*

CHARMAINE. The money is yours?

ANNIE. Ah, well yes and no. I haven't told you everything and it's really better if you don't know.

CHARMAINE. So there's more going on here than just trying to get rid of Mr. Davis?

ANNIE. You could say that.

CHARMAINE. Does it have to do with the money?

ANNIE. You could say that.

GEORGE. *(Sets the bag on the end table and begins to pace.)* OK, someone moved the money from your bag into Marilena's and only one person, besides the second ghost, went into the kitchen where I left the bag.

ANNIE. Bernard!

GEORGE. *(Stops pacing.)* We can't do business with a thief.

CHARMAINE. Hold on, are you saying that Bernard stole your money?

GEORGE. Absolutely.

CHARMAINE. Then why not just turn him over to the police?

ANNIE. Ah, well, there's a slight problem with that…you see…we're not exactly squeaky clean ourselves.

CHARMAINE. Are you telling me that money was obtained illegally?

ANNIE. Oh no!

CHARMAINE. Are you telling me that the money was not obtained illegally?

ANNIE. No.

CHARMAINE. What are you telling me?

ANNIE. I'm telling you, that I did not tell you that the money was obtained illegally.

GEORGE. What are we going to do?

CHARMAINE. Can I help?

ANNIE. Only if you don't ask any more questions about the money.

CHARMAINE. I never was very good at twenty questions. It sounds like Mr. Oppenheimer is as crooked as a three dollar bill. Count me in. Sorority sisters unite!

ANNIE. We have to find a way to expose him. Wait a minute, wait a minute. Dad, do you remember when I answered his phone when we were tangled up on the bed?

GEORGE. Sure, why?

ANNIE. Well, I didn't think much about it at the time, but now the message I was told to give him is making sense. It was something about they're closing in and it's time to move. Bernard said it had to do with the stock market, but that doesn't make a lot of sense.

CHARMAINE. I was in this television show once, and they were able to get a lot of information about a possible suspect from his cell phone. Bernard seems awful connected to his. Maybe we could find some information that would help you get something on him. Why, he's already proven he's not Mr. Clean.

GEORGE. I like that, but how do we get our hands on his cell phone.

CHARMAINE. That's where I come in honey lamb. Y'all just leave him to me. His ass is grass and I'm the lawnmower.

ANNIE. What do you have in mind?

CHARMAINE. Why when a man thinks he's going to the Promised Land his engine is running but ain't nobody drivin'. I'll get that phone and he won't know what's happened to him. Just give me a few minutes to freshen up and I'll be good to go. *(Exits to bedroom one.)*

GEORGE. *(Sits on the couch right side.)* I can believe that. You know Annie, I really am too old for all this intrigue. I think I've developed tennis elbow.

ANNIE. Dad, you've never played tennis in your life.

GEORGE. Well, alright then, printing press elbow.

ANNIE. There's no such thing as printing press elbow.

GEORGE. There is now. I'm the first.

ANNIE. Rheumatoid arthritis, sciatica, lumbago, asthma, bunions, shin splints, blood pressure or printing press elbow, you'll always be first with me Dad. *(Kisses him on the cheek.)* So, maybe we should just give it all up and retire.

GEORGE. I've always thought retiring to a ranch would be nice. Which reminds me, did I ever tell you the joke about the three sons on a cattle ranch in Montana?

ANNIE. Dad, what could possibly be funny about a cattle ranch in Montana?

GEORGE. It's not really a joke, it's a three word pun, I'm sure you'll enjoy it.

ANNIE. *(Resigned to listening, sits in the chair.)* Alright, let's hear it.

GEORGE. OK here we go. There's a widow in New Hampshire...

ANNIE. I thought you said it was a cattle ranch in Montana.

GEORGE. It will be in a minute if you give me a chance.

ANNIE. Sorry Dad.

GEORGE. OK, here we go again. There's a widow in New Jersey...

ANNIE. I thought you said New Hampshire.

GEORGE. It doesn't matter. New Hampshire, New Jersey, New Zealand.

ANNIE. Can you get on with the story?

GEORGE. OK, here we go…again. There's a widow in New York… *(Pauses and looks at* **ANNIE** *to see if she is going to interrupt.)* and she wants her boys to have a better life and a better opportunity than she did. So she scrimps and saves and eventually has enough money to buy them a cattle ranch in Montana, and off the boys go. Sometime later, she is on the phone to them, asking how it's going. They respond, "Great, we just have one problem, we don't know what to call the ranch." She replies, "That's easy, you must call it the Prism ranch." They say, "Why?" She says, "Because that's where: The Sons *(Suns.)* Raise *(Rays.)* Meat *(Meet.).*

ANNIE. *(After a long pause.)* I don't get it.

GEORGE. Annie, think about it…it's a three word pun, The Sons Raise Meat.

ANNIE. I know that Dad, it's a cattle ranch.

GEORGE. Annie, it's a good thing I love you.

ANNIE. I love you too Dad.

BERNARD. *(Enters from bedroom two followed by* **BUD.***)* Sorry about the bad news Bud, I'll see you later.

(Looks at **MARILENA***'s bag, still on the end table, then exits up left, but returns, and hiding behind the corner, just visible to the audience but unseen by the others, listens and watches.)*

BUD. *(Moves downstage.)* Hi, you two have a minute?

GEORGE. *(Stands.)* Come and sit down

ANNIE. *(Stands.)* Certainly. What can we do for you? *(She moves to the couch left side.)*

BUD. *(Sits in the chair.)* Well I just got the numbers from Bernard and quite frankly, they are higher than I expected. In fact, my idea of a retirement home is totally out of the question.

ANNIE. Does that mean you no longer want this place?

BUD. I don't know what I want.

(**CHARMAINE** *appears in the doorway of bedroom one now wearing a low cut blouse, skirt and heels and looking very glamorous. She stops and listens.*)

I think I'm getting too old to continue chasing chicks, and Marilena has convinced me that it's just too dangerous. I'm not as quick as I used to be. I think perhaps it's time for me to settle down.

(**CHARMAINE** *reacts.*)

ANNIE. Would you be willing to entertain a serious offer on the manor?

BUD. I think I might. Why don't you make me one and I'll look at it.

ANNIE. Thank you. Dad, why don't we go into the kitchen and get out the appraisal documents and our offer. We'll get it to you shortly Bud.

(**ANNIE** *takes the bag, hands it to* **GEORGE**.)

Dad, you'd better take this downstairs.

(**BERNARD**, *still watching, reacts then exits up left.* **ANNIE** *and* **GEORGE** *exit to the kitchen.*)

CHARMAINE. (*Moves downstage towards* **BUD**.) Budly, my, my, why you look like you've been chewed up and spit out.

BUD. Well I've not had the best of news, but perhaps it is for the best.

CHARMAINE. Bud, I couldn't help but overhear your conversation earlier. Did you mean that?

BUD. What?

CHARMAINE. You know, giving up your profession as a chick chaser and settling down?

BUD. Me, a chick chaser?

CHARMAINE. What would you call it?

BUD. Well, I can't help myself. All my life I've been like a bee in a garden of beautiful flowers. (*Pauses, stands and moves towards* **CHARMAINE**.) If only I could find a queen to settle down with. My Cherie, you look as lovely as a magnolia blossom in the spring time.

CHARMAINE. Why you silver tongued fox. I've kinda missed you. *(Kisses him on the cheek.)*

BUD. Maybe you won't have to miss me. Perhaps we should reacquaint ourselves, with a moonlight rendezvous.

CHARMAINE. Why my Budly Studly, you still are quick with your moves. But this time, I need a little more than just roses, wine, and empty promises before you get to the Promised Land. Speaking of which…er…well… there's a little thing I have to do, but after that I would love to hear all about how you plan to settle down.

ANNIE. *(Enters from the kitchen, with a bunch of papers in her hand. She hands the papers to BUD.)* Here you are Bud. There's a valuation of the manor, and I think you will like our offer.

BUD. Thank you, I promise you I will look it over carefully. Until later my *petit chou (Bows and kisses CHARMAINE's hand and exits to the bedroom two.)*

ANNIE. *(Crosses to CHARMAINE.)* You and Bud? I thought he was as welcome as a skunk at a lawn party?

CHARMAINE. I know a leopard doesn't change its spots, but, just maybe, this leopard can be tamed. With all the magic happening around here, who knows?

ANNIE. But what about Bernard?

CHARMAINE. Sister, don't you worry, I still plan on getting that phone.

ANNIE. Good luck.

CHARMAINE. *(Adjusts her dress and hitches up her bra.)* Luck ain't got nothin' to do with it. Now you two stand by in the kitchen, I'll get you that phone, but you're going to have to move quickly to get what information you can from it. I won't be able to keep him away from it for very long.

ANNIE. You've got it.

CHARMAINE. Here he comes, quick. (**ANNIE** *exits to the kitchen.*)

BERNARD. (*Enters from upstage left, talking on his phone.*) Right, I know… I've got one more thing I have to do then…(*Sees* **CHARMAINE**.) I can't talk now, I'll have to call you back. (*Puts the cell phone in his shirt pocket and moves downstage.*) Hello.

CHARMAINE. Hello handsome.

BERNARD. (*Looks around.*) Me?

CHARMAINE. Ain't nobody else here, except maybe a ghost or two.

(**BERNARD** *begins walking around the couch looking for* **MARILENA***'s bag, followed closely by* **CHARMAINE***. He bends down and starts looking under the couch.* **CHARMAINE** *bends over to see what he's looking at.*)

Looking for something? Anything I can help you find?

BERNARD. (*Slowly straightens up and finds his face about an inch from her bosom.*) I think I just found them.

CHARMAINE. They were never lost.

(*She straightens up, followed by* **BERNARD**.)

Now, why don't you come sit down right next to little ol' me and relax a little.

(*She pushes him onto the couch middle and sits close to him on the right.* **BERNARD** *inches away left.* **CHARMAINE** *inches left.* **BERNARD** *inches away left followed by* **CHARMAINE** *until he is against the arm of the sofa.* **CHARMAINE** *leans over and runs her fingers through his hair.* **ANNIE** *peeks out from the kitchen door as* **BERNARD***'s cell phone rings.* **CHARMAINE** *takes it out of his shirt pocket and answers.*)

Hello, B.O.'s not here.

(*She hangs up the phone. With the phone in her left hand, she leans into* **BERNARD** *with the phone behind his head.* **ANNIE** *grabs it from her and hands it to* **GEORGE** *who has appeared in the doorway and they* *quickly retreat into the kitchen.* **BERNARD** *reaches right to grab* **CHARMAINE**. *Her manner changes as she backs away.)*

CHARMAINE. *(cont.)* You know Bernard, us southern gals like to be romanced. Why a perfect place would be that lovely garden of Annie's, don't you think?

*(***BERNARD*** *simply nods his head yes as* **CHARMAINE** *grabs him by the tie, and leads him out through the French doors.)*

*(***ANNIE*** *enters followed by* **GEORGE** *carrying Bernard's phone. She quickly moves up to the book case and grabs the computer.)*

ANNIE. OK Dad, let's see what we can find on the phone and I'll record the information.

(They move left to the table and sit as Bernard's phone rings.)

*(***GEORGE*** *looks at the phone and* **ANNIE** *signals to him to answer it.* **GEORGE** *imitates Bernard's voice.)*

GEORGE. Hello, B.O. here. Yes... O.K... Right... Will do, bye.

ANNIE. Who was that?

GEORGE. *(Looking at the phone.)* It was from a David Olsen. He said "hey bro" and called me Brian.

ANNIE. What? Are you sure you heard that correctly?

GEORGE. I'm not deaf. He said, "hey bro" and called me Brian.

ANNIE. *(Slowly.)* So, Bernard Oppenheimer is really Brian Olsen? Why is he calling himself Bernard?

GEORGE. Sounds rather shifty to me, something is rotten in Denmark.

ANNIE. Well we only have a short time with the phone, so let's get all the information we can. *(Voices off in the garden.)* Come on Dad, we can finish this in the kitchen.

(They exit quickly to the kitchen with the computer and phone.)

*(***CHARMAINE*** *enters from the French doors with* ***BERNARD***. *They stop just inside the French doors and* ***CHARMAINE*** *kisses him full on the lips as* ***BUD*** *opens his door and sees them then quickly retreats and closes the door.)*

CHARMAINE. Why don't you meet me in this bedroom *(Points to the room.)* in ten minutes honey lamb.

*(***BERNARD***, *with his mouth wide open just nods and exits up left.* ***CHARMAINE*** *moves quickly to the kitchen door.)*

Annie, George?

*(***ANNIE*** *and* ***GEORGE*** *enter.)*

Listen right now I've got him mesmerized, but sooner or later he's going to want what I've been promising, as well as his phone back. How much longer do you need?

ANNIE. We've got something really good, but a little more time would be helpful. We're still looking at his previous calls. He sure does use the phone a lot.

GEORGE. Are you going to be alright?

CHARMAINE. Don't you worry about me. I can handle that lower than a snake's belly in a wagon rut thief. But how do I get the phone back?

ANNIE. As soon as we're done, I'll put it on the end table.

(She exits to the kitchen followed by ***GEORGE*** *as* ***BUD*** *enters from bedroom two.)*

BUD. There you arc you...you... Delilah, you Benedict Arnold, you...you Jezebel. *(Crosses down stage center.)*

CHARMAINE. *(Crosses left toward* ***BUD***.*)* Why sugar pie, whatever are you talkin' about? Why you look angrier than a hell and damnation preacher with a burr in his saddle.

BUD. *(Exaggerating his imitation of* **CHARMAINE** *in movement and voice.)* "I need a little more than just roses, wine, and empty promises before you get to the Promised Land." "Why I would love to hear all about how you plan to settle down." I just bet you would, and then make a fool of me later.

CHARMAINE. But I do want to hear…

BUD. I saw you kissing Bernard.

CHARMAINE. Why bless your pea picking little heart, you're jealous. But you have to believe me Budly Studly, I wasn't kissin' him, he was kissin' me. Why, he forced his attentions on me. The only one I want kissin' me is you!

(**CHARMAINE** *gives him a big kiss.*)

BUD. Why that dirty dog. I have a mind to fire him right now.

CHARMAINE. Oh, Budly, I don't want to get anyone in trouble. I'd feel ever so bad if someone lost their job because of me. Maybe you could just keep a watch out for him and make sure I'm never alone with him.

BUD. *(Flexes his muscles.)* Your Studly Budly do-right is on the job. If he thinks he can pull the wool over my eyes, he has another think coming. I'll watch him like a hawk, and if he tries to make a move on my beautiful Southern Belle. I'll squash him like a little bug.

CHARMAINE. Oh my, you've got my engine running. Now why don't you just let me slip into something comfortable and I'll meet you in my bedroom in say five minutes? *(Exits to bedroom one.)*

BUD. I will be counting the moments.

(He follows her to the bottom of the stairs and blows her a kiss as **MARILENA** *enters through the French Doors with an umbrella, which she shakes off and closes. She sees* **BUD** *and advances towards him. He turns, sees her and immediately puts his hand over his crotch and starts to back up the stairs to escape.* **MARILENA** *uses her umbrella as a bar behind him and stops his retreat.)*

BUD. *(cont.)* Stay away from me.

> (**CHARMAINE**, *hearing* **BUD**'s *voice, opens her door and watches as* **BUD** *quickly moves back down the stairs and crosses downstage left to the table followed by* **MARILENA** *with the table between them.*)

What do you want? Go away!

MARILENA. *Imi pare rau, iarta-ma te rog. [See Authors' Notes.] (I'm sorry, forgive me please.)*

BUD. What are you saying? Are you casting a spell on me?

> (**BUD**, *again holding his crotch, crosses right in front of the couch followed my* **MARILENA**.)

MARILENA. No, please, listen to me. The first time I uh… you know…came across your gentleman's department was deliberate, the second time was accidental. I want you…

BUD. To stay away from my gentleman's department.

CHARMAINE. *(Has come down and is now standing at the foot of the steps.)* Oh Bud, I'm so proud of you.

> (**BUD** *seizes the opportunity to escape from* **MARILENA** *and runs up to* **CHARMAINE**'s *left, who turns to* **MARILENA**.)

You, you should be ashamed of yourself chasing after my Budly Studly. Why he's a pillar of virtue.

BUD. I am?

CHARMAINE. Tell her you're a new man.

BUD. I'm a new man.

MARILENA. That is good to hear. All I wanted to do was apologize for earlier. It appears the spirits have forgiven and I must too.

BUD. Fine, but just keep that thing *(Points at the umbrella.)* away from me.

MARILENA. *(Floats up towards* **BUD** *waving the umbrella around.)* The vibrations are strong.

(**BUD** *backs away right almost pushing* **CHARMAINE** *till she is right outside the kitchen door.*)

MARILENA. *(cont.)* Speak to me spirits, let me enter your world.

BUD. I wish you would.

MARILENA. Shhsh…the spirits are angry.

(*She is now close to* **BUD** *who escapes by climbing over the back of the couch, then goes up to the foot of the stairs.*)

Peace be with you spirits.

(*She is still waving the umbrella and* **BUD** *keeps his distance.*)

CHARMAINE. (*Gently puts a hand on the umbrella, and keeps it motionless.*) I'm sure Marilena doesn't mean you any harm Bud, do you Marilena?

MARILENA. Of course not, it's just that the spirits seem restless.

CHARMAINE. Bud, I'm fixin' to have you and Marilena make up, so why don't you just shake hands with her and forgive and forget?

BUD. (*Slowly and cautiously inches right towards* **MARILENA.**) Well OK

(*He puts out his hand towards* **MARILENA,** *as* **GEORGE** *enters from the kitchen. The door hits* **CHARMAINE,** *who staggers into* **MARILENA** *who staggers left and hits* **BUD** *in the crotch with the umbrella. Everyone stands stock still and looks at* **BUD,** *who gives a silent scream of agony and stands motionless holding his crotch. Then his knees slowly buckle and he collapses to the floor.*)

CHARMAINE. (*Kneels down next to him.*) Oh my poor Budly, I sure do hope there's no permanent damage.

BUD. Oh-Oh-Oh.

MARILENA. I'm so sorry.

BUD. Oh-Oh-Oh.

GEORGE. Are you alright Mr. Davis?

BUD. Oh-Oh-Oh. I think some ice might be a good idea.

MARILENA. *(Takes one step left towards* **CHARMAINE** *and* **BUD**.*)* Let me help you.

BUD. No – No. Stay away from me. *(He gets up carefully keeping* **CHARMAINE** *between himself and* **MARILENA**.*)* I'll get it myself. *(He limps into the kitchen.)*

GEORGE. Marilena, why don't I take you home?

MARILENA. Oh thank you George.

> *(They head towards the French doors.)*

You know I really didn't do anything.

> *(She makes a movement with the umbrella.)*

GEORGE. I know my dear, – er – er, why don't I carry the umbrella?

> *(He takes it from her and they exit the French doors.)*

CHARMAINE. That's a great idea George. *(Turns toward the kitchen door.)*

BERNARD. *(Enters from up left, now dressed in a crew neck T-Shirt and lounge pants.)* Ah, Ms. Beauregard, *(He comes down to her with outstretched arms.)* Um, er, you haven't seen my phone have you?

CHARMAINE. *(Turns and kisses him full on the lips.)* How can you think of phones at a time like this? Why, I could take that personally.

BERNARD. I'm sorry. It's just that – You're right of course. *(He opens the bedroom door and holds it for her.)* Shall we?

CHARMAINE. Why, you're such a gentleman, are you sure you're not from The South?

BERNARD. Right now I'm not sure where I'm from, I don't think I can even remember my name.

CHARMAINE. *(Closes the door and strikes a sexy pose.)* I often have that effect on men. Now, you get into bed.

> *(He leaps onto the bed.)*

There's something I just have to get from my room. Don't be going anywhere honey lamb *(She exits the bedroom, closes the door and leans on it.)* Now What?

(She holds open the kitchen door. **BUD** *limps out still holding his crotch.)*

CHARMAINE. *(cont.)* Oh my poor Budly. *(Calling through the door.)* Annie, can you speed things up, I can't hold him up much longer.

BUD. Really I'm OK. You don't have to hold me up at all.

CHARMAINE. You sure?

*(***BUD*** *nods yes.)*

Well then, don't you be too far away, in case that Mr. Oppenheimer, wants to force his attentions on me.

BUD. Never fear my dear. Your Budly Studly will be ready willing and able to deal with that interloper. But I think I'll just lie down on the couch for a few minutes.

*(***CHARMAINE*** *helps him onto the couch, then tip toes behind the couch, silently opens the bedroom door, deliberately makes sure it stays open, and steps into the room in a sexy manner.* **BERNARD** *sits up, his mouth wide open and watches as* **CHARMAINE** *slowly unbuttons her blouse. She then flings herself on the bed on top of* **BERNARD**, *then quickly moves so he is on top and she is underneath.)*

BERNARD. You're amazing.

CHARMAINE. True.

BERNARD. Are you always like this?

CHARMAINE. *(In a loud and exaggerated manner.)* No Bernard, no.

BUD. *(Leaps to his feet and rushes into the bedroom.)* Mr. Oppenheimer, when a lady says no, she means no. Now stop. Leave her alone.

*(***CHARMAINE*** *stands up and closes her blouse.)*

I have a mind to fire you right now. Charmaine, are you alright?

CHARMAINE. *(Runs to* **BUD**.*)* I'm fine, no harm done. Please don't fire him over little ol' me.

BERNARD. Mr. Davis you've got it all wrong. It's not me, it's her.

BUD. That's ridiculous.

CHARMAINE. Bud, you were supposed to be restin'. Now, why don' t you just let me help you to your room and then I'll come and check on you in a few minutes.

*(She helps the still wobbly **BUD** up to bedroom two, as **BERNARD** watches from the bedroom doorway. **BUD** exits, **CHARMAINE** turns and comes back down.)*

There's just too much going on out here.

(She gives him a little kiss.)

My room. Five minutes. Be there. *(Starts towards bedroom one.)*

BERNARD. *(To himself.)* My, my, what a woman. *(Turns and goes into the bathroom.)*

ANNIE. *(Enters from the kitchen with her computer and sees **CHARMAINE**.)* Hi, how's it going?

CHARMAINE. I can't hold him off much longer.

ANNIE. You don't have to, we've got him, just look.

*(**ANNIE** holds out the computer towards **CHARMAINE**.)*

CHARMAINE. Look at what? It's blank.

ANNIE. My computer must have died and my charger's in my room. Come on, I'll tell you about it while I get my cord. Just wait till you see what we found. Here, *(Hands **CHARMAINE** the phone.)* you can give him his phone back.

*(**ANNIE** exits up left followed by **CHARMAINE**.)*

*(**BERNARD** comes out of the bedroom just in time to see **ANNIE** and **CHARMAINE** exit. He looks furtively around, and quickly moves towards the kitchen. He slowly peeks into the kitchen, realizes no one is there, and quickly exits into the kitchen seen by **GEORGE** who has just entered from the French doors. **GEORGE** crosses right, peeks in the kitchen then turns as **ANNIE** and **CHARMAINE** re-appear from up left.)*

ANNIE. *(cont.)* Dad, I'm so glad you're back, just wait till you see what I've got to show you. *(She moves down to the table, plugs her computer into a wall socket then sits.)* I think you should both be sitting down for this.

(GEORGE *and* **CHARMAINE** *sit at the table.)*

Tell you what, I'm enjoying this so much, why don't I just read it to you. It's an article from the Tampa Bay Chronicle dated about three weeks ago. *(Reading.)* "The Sarasota County Sheriff's department today issued warrants for the arrest of the Olsen brothers. David and Brian Olsen are charged with defrauding several local banks by obtaining mortgages with inflated house evaluations. They allegedly made several million dollars by flipping properties between three different companies they owned. They fled the area and their whereabouts are unknown. Anyone with information regarding these two should contact the Sarasota County Sheriff's Office."

GEORGE. Bingo!

CHARMAINE. Why that connivin' snake in the grass! I should have known. How could I have been so blind.

GEORGE. That reminds me, did I ever tell you the joke about the blind man?

ANNIE. Dad, we don't have time for jokes.

CHARMAINE. Well I would love to hear the joke.

GEORGE. See Annie, some people like jokes.

ANNIE. Just get on with it Dad.

GEORGE. OK here we go. There's this beautiful young housewife, who always does her housework naked.

CHARMAINE. Well bless my stars and garters, so do I.

GEORGE. Really?

CHARMAINE. Uh, huh.

ANNIE. Dad!

GEORGE. OK, so she's naked in the house and the doorbell rings. She goes to the door and calls through the door. "Who is it?" A voice says, "It's the blind man."

She thinks, "That's alright," then opens the door and says, "Come in." He steps into the room while she closes the door. She says, "What can I do for you?" He says, "Wow, I suppose you could tell me where to hang the blinds."

(**ANNIE** *looks blank as* **CHARMAINE** *begins to giggle.*)

CHARMAINE. Oh Georgie, that's so cute.

ANNIE. I don't get it.

GEORGE. Never mind Annie. Let's get back to the Olsen brothers. What are we going to do?

ANNIE. Well, it seems to me we might just be able to make a deal. Does anyone know where BO is right now?

GEORGE. He's in the basement and we all know what he's doing down there. He's gone for the money again.

ANNIE. Dad, is the backdoor open?

GEORGE. Yes. If we don't stop him, he'll be long gone.

CHARMAINE. Whatever would y'all do without me? He'd never leave without this. (*Holds up the phone.*) I'll go fetch that varmint quicker than green grass through a goose. Then you can make your deal. (*Exits to the kitchen setting the phone on the end table.*)

GEORGE. This means I'm going to be back in the dungeon again. I can feel my sciatica starting up.

ANNIE. Dad, you'll be fine. As a matter of fact I've noticed a little spring in your step today. It wouldn't have anything to do with the "Romanian fruitcake" would it?

GEORGE. Annie, she is The Contesa Marilena de Buzau Si Severin, to you. And she happens to be a very sweet lady.

ANNIE. So…

GEORGE. So, it's none of your business.

(**CHARMAINE** *enters from the kitchen followed by* **BERNARD** *who is carrying the money bag.*)

CHARMAINE. Why Georgie and Annie, what a surprise.

BERNARD. *(Quickly tries to hide the bag behind his back.)* Er… er…yes, what a surprise.

*(**BERNARD***'s phone rings. She quickly walks over to the end table, picks it up and holds it to her ear with a flourish and mimics his sing-song manner.)*

CHARMAINE. Hello Brian Olsen.

(There is a stunned silence as she hands him the phone.)

My work is done here, I'm going to go see how my Budly is doing. *(Exits to bedroom two.)*

BERNARD. I can't talk now. *(Hangs up and puts the phone in his pocket.)*

ANNIE. What? At a loss for words?

GEORGE. Cat got your tongue?

BERNARD. We need to talk.

ANNIE. I'll do the talking, you do the listening. Here's the deal. We do not call the Sarasota County Sheriff's Office, and you disappear out of our lives forever, right now! Take it or leave it.

BERNARD. I'll take it. I'll just get my things and be out of here. *(Heads up left.)*

GEORGE. Mr. Olsen

*(**GEORGE** points to the money bag, then indicates to place it on the floor. **BERNARD** looks at **GEORGE**, then at **ANNIE**, then at the money bag. He drops the bag on the floor and exits up left.)*

*(**ANNIE** goes to get the bag and takes it back to the table, as **MARILENA** enters through the French doors, sobbing.)*

Marilena my dear, what's wrong? Come, please sit down.

MARILENA. No, no, I can't sit.

*(She begins to move around the room still sobbing with **GEORGE** trying to keep up with her.)*

Please, you must forgive me. I have done something terrible.

GEORGE. Marilena…

MARILENA. No, let me finish, please. At the séance tonight, I did something awful. I was so afraid that my psychic powers would let me down, and I wanted to please you so much, that I hired a friend of mine to masquerade as a ghost. I couldn't live with myself, if I didn't confess this to you. I was so stupid, because as it turns out, my powers did not fail me, there was a real spirit after all.

ANNIE. Marilena, there's something that we…

GEORGE. Want to thank you for. It was your psychic powers that delivered us our ghost. Isn't that right Annie?

ANNIE. *(Pauses for a moment frowning at* **GEORGE***.)* That's right Dad.

GEORGE. It all worked out in the end, so of course we forgive you.

MARILENA. *(Rushes into* **GEORGE***'s arms and gives him a kiss.) Multumesc. [See Authors' Notes.]* Thank you.

GEORGE. Listen my dear, why don't you scoot back home and I'll come over in just a little while. There are a few things I'd like to talk to you about.

MARILENA. Over dinner?

GEORGE. You cook?

MARILENA. I love to cook.

GEORGE. Really? I didn't think anyone cooked these days, I thought it was just something you watched on T.V.

MARILENA. I wasn't planning on watching T.V. tonight George. *La revadere.*

(She kisses **GEORGE** *again, spins around, then floats out the French doors.)*

(Enter **CHARMAINE** *followed by* **BUD** *from bedroom two in unusually close proximity because* **BUD***'s sweater vest is caught in the back of* **CHARMAINE***'s skirt zipper. They shuffle down the stairs and stop at the bottom as* **CHARMAINE** *tries to adjust her skirt, which has risen up. As she does this,* **BUD** *follows her every move.)*

GEORGE. What are you two doing?

BUD. Ah, er…well, you see my vest seems to be caught in her zipper.

(**GEORGE** *moves left and walks around them, inspecting the situation as* **CHARMAINE** *continues to wiggle and* **BUD** *follows her moves.*)

GEORGE. How in heaven's name did you ever get into this mess?

ANNIE. *(Still sitting at the table.)* Please don't answer that question.

BUD. We just got caught up in the moment.

CHARMAINE. He was feeling a little bit low.

BUD. I was just trying to give you a hand.

CHARMAINE. Can somebody please do somethin'?

ANNIE. I'll get some scissors. *(Exits to the kitchen.)*

GEORGE. Here, let me see if I can get it.

(He reaches between the two of them and starts to make faces as he begins to tug on the zipper.)

I'd thought I'd seen it all, but…

CHARMAINE. Please don't use the word butt.

BUD. Watch where you're putting your hands buddy.

GEORGE. Sorry. *(He steps back and surveys the situation.)* Well, your vest can't go down and neither can her skirt, that means Charmaine's skirt has to go up.

BUD. Good idea.

CHARMAINE. I don't think that's going to work.

BUD. Well, we could at least try.

CHARMAINE. Alright Georgie, go ahead, but no peekin'.

*(**GEORGE** takes **CHARMAINE**'s skirt and lifts it until it gets stuck under her bosom, but is covering her face. He continues to try to tug it up. Her underwear is revealed [See Authors' Notes.], as **ANNIE** enters from the kitchen with a pair of scissors in her hand.)*

ANNIE. Dad, you just got busted.

GEORGE. For someone with no sense of humor Annie, that's not bad.

ANNIE. You can let go now Dad.

*(***GEORGE*** *let's go and lowers the skirt.)*

Okay, let's see what I can do.

*(She moves behind ***CHARMAINE***, clicking the scissors.)*

BUD. What are you going to do?

ANNIE. I'm just going to snip a little off.

BUD. Not to me you're not!

CHARMAINE. Be careful Annie, I need my Budly Studly intact.

ANNIE. OK, hold still. *(She cuts and they break apart.)*

CHARMAINE. Thanks Annie. I want you to know that Bud isn't interested in buying the manor. It's all yours, and with the money from the sale, we're going to go on a world cruise. It will be hard for him to get away from me on a ship, don't you think? He tells me we are going to make beautiful music together. Isn't that right Budly?

BUD. Oh yes my love, it is true. You have the face that launched a thousand ships, Helen of Troy. You have the body of the Venus de Milo, and clearly the mind and spirit of Cleopatra. I am yours forever.

*(He takes ***CHARMAINE*** in his arms. As they turn we see for the first time a large hole cut in the rear of ***CHARMAINE****'s skirt revealing underwear.* ***BUD*** *takes his hand and purposely covers the hole as they waltz out through the French doors.)*

ANNIE. So Dad, are you and Marilena going to make beautiful music together?

GEORGE. Speaking of beautiful music, did I ever tell you about the group of tourists who visited Beethoven's grave in Germany?

ANNIE. Dad, it's getting late. Don't you think we've all had enough of your jokes today?

GEORGE. Well, maybe, how about just one more.

ANNIE. Alright, I'm listening.

GEORGE. OK, here goes. There's a group of tourists visiting Beethoven's grave in a small town in Germany. As they stand by the tombstone, they hear music. It's Beethoven's Fifth symphony being played backwards. Someone asks, "What is this weird music?" The guide says, "Oh, don't worry, it's just Beethoven. He's decomposing."

ANNIE. *(There is a long pause as her face remains blank. Then slowly her face begins to change as her eyes light up and she begins to smile.)* Composing...decomposing... Oh Dad, I get it. *(She begins to giggle.)* Beethoven, composing... decomposing.

(She starts to laugh hysterically as **GEORGE** *kisses her on the head and exits out the French doors.)*

(Curtain.)

FURNITURE AND PROPERTY LIST

ON STAGE

A double bed with pillows and bedspread.

Two bedside tables.

Sofa with cushions.

Low back easy chair.

End table. ON IT: Magazines.

Round Table. ON IT: Money, some loose. Some money
    stacks rubber banded. Loose rubber bands.

Two chairs.

Books.

Lap top computer.

Delta MU bag.

ACT I OFFSTAGE

Oil can. (**GEORGE**.)

Charmaine's suitcase. (**GEORGE**.)

Delta MU bag. IN IT: Bra and panties.(**CHARMAINE**.)

Tray with sandwiches. Pot of coffee. Three mugs. (**ANNIE**.)

Wine. Chocolates. (**BUD**.)

One super sized bath towel. (**GEORGE** and **CHARMAINE**.)

Bottle of wine. Two wine glasses. (**BUD**.)

Spray bottle of perfume. (**CHARMAINE**.)

Bottle of wine. Two glasses. (**GEORGE**.)

Small to medium size zipper travel bag. In it: Round
    tablecloth. Electric Candle. (**MARILENA**.)

Two folding chairs. (**GEORGE**.)

One folding chair. (**MARILENA**.)

Handcuffs. (**BUD**.)

ACT II OFFSTAGE

Large umbrella. (**MARILENA.**)
Business papers. (**BERNARD.**)
Business papers. (**ANNIE.**)
Scissors. (**ANNIE.**)

PERSONAL

Cell phone. (**BERNARD.**)
Notepad. Pencil. (**BERNARD.**)
Electronic stud finder. (**BERNARD.**)
Bendable tape measure. (**BERNARD.**)
Pill bottle with blue pills. (**BUD.**)

COSTUMES

ANNIE	**GEORGE**
Blue jeans or blue jean skirt.	Checkered shirt.
Blouse.	Overalls.
Casual shoes.	Tool belt.
	Work boots.
	T-shirt.
	Yellow smiley face boxers.

CHARMAINE	**MARILENA**
Low cut summer dress.	Peasant blouse.
Matching purse.	Long skirt.
High heel shoes.	Head scarf.
Dressy robe.	Sandals.
Sensuous sleepwear.	Short evening gown.
Skirt with cut out rear.	Tiara.
Blouse.	High heel shoes.
Sandals.	Raincoat.
	Negligee.

BUD
Short Sleeve plaid shirt.
Khaki pants.
Sweater vest.
Golf cap.
Socks.
Tennis shoes.
Boxers with red hearts.
Silk like robe.
Scarf *(Cravat.)*.
T-shirt.

BERNARD
Button down shirt with tie.
Khaki pants.
Socks.
Dress shoes.
Crew neck T-shirt.
Lounge pants.
Flip flops.
Belt.

AUTHORS' NOTES

In the authors' experience, there are people who can tell jokes, and there are people who can not. It does not seem to be something that can be taught or learned. We recommend that part of the audition process for the role of George, be the telling of a joke.

Page 34. A thin, ie. ½ in or less, metal tape, flexible enough to bend easily, works well, or a very long fabric tape,

Page 53. Clock wise from 12 o'clock to eight o'clock: Annie, George, Marilena, Bernard and Bud.

Page 54. At this point, as George dims the lights, we need almost total darkness in the area of the bookcase. Just enough light in the center stage area to see the action, and, of course the candlelight on the table.

Page 55. The entrance cues for the two ghosts will obviously depend on the size of the auditorium, and the time taken to climb onto the stage. Suffice to say that the audience should be able, albeit briefly, to see both at the same time.

Page 84. The authors deliberately do not describe "underwear", leaving it to the individual theatres to decide how conservative, or not, would be appropriate for their audiences.

ROMANIAN PRONUNCIATION

Page 11. Boozoh she Severeen.

Page 14. Boonah sarah.

Page 14. Lah reevuhdairy.

Page 21. Oh doeamny.

Page 22. Ah-oh-lew.

Page 22. My Terzyou.

Page 30. Sunt eenca yo.

Page 31. Cred kuh imi plach.

Page 75. Imi pareh ro, yarta muh te rogue.

Page 83. Mulchewmesk.

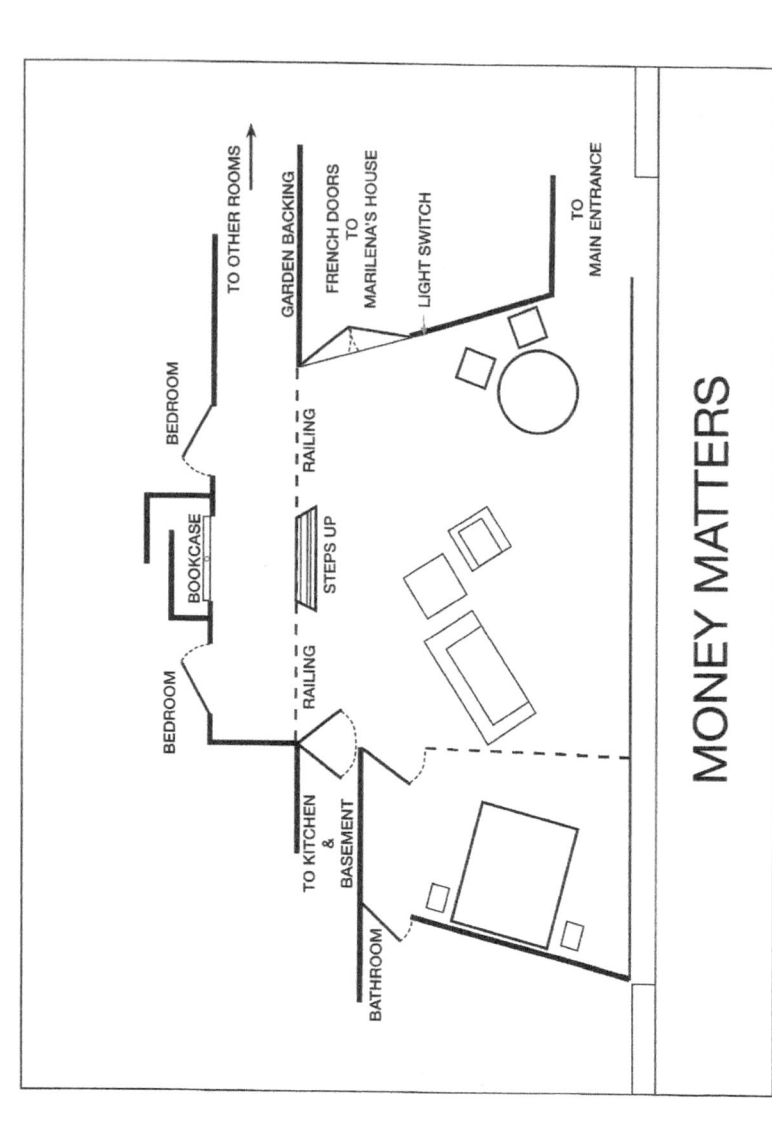

GARDEN BACKING

FRENCH DOORS
TO
MARILENA'S HOUSE

LIGHT SWITCH

TO OTHER ROOMS

BEDROOM

BOOKCASE

RAILING

STEPS UP

BEDROOM

RAILING

TO KITCHEN
&
BASEMENT

BATHROOM

TO
MAIN ENTRANCE

MONEY MATTERS